MANHATTAN
LULLABY

MANHATTAN LULLABY

A Novel of Love in New York

GLYNNIS WALKER WRITING AS

OLIVIA DE GROVE

Copyright © 1989 by Olivia De Grove

Cover design by Kat JK Lee

ISBN: 978-1-5040-1396-3

Distributed in 2015 by Open Road Distribution
345 Hudson Street
New York, NY 10014
www.openroadmedia.com

To Sabrina,
"A gentle nymph that sways
the smooth Severn stream."

MANHATTAN
LULLABY

PART ONE

Hel-lo Ba-by!

CHAPTER ONE

DEAR MAXINE,

I don't usually write to advice columnists, but I have a problem which I can't really discuss with my friends because it's a little, well, weird is the word, I suppose. So, since I read your column in Destiny magazine every month and you seem to get some fairly outrageous letters, I thought maybe you might be able to handle one from me.

My husband and I have been married for five-and-a-half years. In the beginning we had a fairly active sex life. I mean actually it was extremely active, hectic even. But about a year ago it seemed to taper off. My husband said he still loved me as much as before, but he needed a little something "extra" to get turned on. I tried to go along with his ideas, and I didn't mind the garter belt and stockings or the fantasies, that kind of stuff. (After all, I grew up in the sixties, so I do have an open mind.) But it's reaching the point where I think things have gone too far.

He recently read somewhere about using whipped cream—you know, spreading it on and then licking it off. I told him he could do it to me but I wouldn't do it to him because of the calories.

Anyway, the next thing you know it was cream cheese. (He says he prefers that because he doesn't really care for sweet things.) And then, he brought home lox. I'm sure you can see where he was heading.

Maxine, I just don't know what to do. He says that playing "Delicatessen," as he likes to call it, is driving him wild. It's just the thing he needs to keep the excitement in our marriage. Last night he wanted to try pastrami with Russian dressing! (I can't even tell you what he had in mind for the pickles!!!) And next he says he wants roast beef with mayonnaise. What am I going to do? You know how hard it is to get Russian dressing out of percale, never mind mayonnaise? So please, tell me, Maxine, what should I do? Tell him to forget it? Find a good laundry? What?

Going Crazy in Cleveland

Maxine Kraft shook her head and picked up a pencil. "Look at it this way, at least you don't have to cook," she wrote in the margin. And then at the bottom of the page she added, "Only kidding, Marge. I'll get to this one in the morning," just in case her secretary found the letter and decided to send it off to typesetting as is. God forbid.

Then she took the letter with the little blue violets running around the border and what looked like a grease spot from a dab of cream cheese in one corner and put it in the "Current" file.

"I wonder if they were kosher pickles."

"If what were kosher pickles?" came a voice from the doorway.

Startled that someone had been listening to her talking to herself, Maxine swiveled her chair around to see who it was. With any luck it wouldn't be someone important. Someone who thought that Dear Maxine—the country's newest advice guru and resident authority on changing social mores—was a real expert and not just a divorced woman in her mid-forties whose husband happened to be the editor-in-charge of the magazine where she worked and who had thought that putting his ex-wife to work was a clever way to get out of paying her support.

But she didn't need to worry. It was no one important. Just Harry. "Oh, it's you." She sounded relieved.

"Who were you expecting? Someone tall, dark and handsome?" Harry was leaning against the doorframe. Watching his ex-wife nattering on to herself reminded him of the old days, the good times before the divorce—long before. Lately it seemed that everything reminded him of something that had gone before. His life had become like summer television. Full of reruns.

"These days I have to watch Tom Selleck to get tall, dark and handsome. But I did think you might be someone about five-eight, smooth-talking and in advertising." She cleared a pile of filing folders off the other chair. "Sit down anyway."

It wasn't much of an invitation, but Harry maneuvered his length into the cramped space that served as Maxine's office. "God, it's a good thing you're not one of those tall, hefty women, otherwise we'd have to get you a bigger office."

"It's a good thing I'm your ex-wife, otherwise you'd have to give me a bigger paycheck too," replied Maxine, who was no fool. "I am developing a very big readership, in case you hadn't noticed."

"Says who?"

Maxine shrugged. "Oh, a little bird told me."

"So Jeffrey Mondavi is still hanging about, is he?" Harry scowled. He hated Jeffrey Mondavi. He was young. He wasn't bad-looking. He had all his hair. And he had his whole life ahead of him.

"Let's just say he keeps finding excuses to drop by. This morning he made a special trip from the twelfth floor just to tell me that advertising rates were going up. I told him I don't care. I don't advertise in Destiny magazine. I just write in it. The man can be a pest . . . But a cute pest."

Harry was nodding his agreement at the "pest" comment, but he stopped in mid-nod when Maxine slid the "cute" part onto the end of her sentence. He had no idea she thought about younger men that way.

Maxine continued. "But then he said that it was my column that was boosting the readership. So of course I let him finish."

"Oh, he did, did he? Well just because he sells advertising space doesn't mean he knows a damn thing about the magazine business."

"I think he likes me."

"Likes you! You probably remind him of his mother. He's about, what, twenty-two, twenty-three?"

"He's twenty-seven." Maxine had already decided that the two decades that separated them was nothing more than a daring difference with perhaps a tinge of wicked waywardness thrown in. And that made her feel good, sophisticated, worldly. Twenty-three years, on the other hand, was too close to one of those words psychiatrists used to describe people with peculiar habits. Like pervert.

"The same age as our son. My point exactly," returned Harry.

"That's not what I meant," replied Maxine through clenched teeth. Sometimes Harry could be so . . . so . . . divorceable! What was wrong with her enjoying a little flirtation with a younger man? It wasn't as though she had any plans to take it further than that. She decided to change the subject lest any more of her developing concepts about her life as a newly single woman came under fire. "About the wedding . . ."

Harry nodded. "Right. I guess we should talk about it. Is everything all set?"

"If you mean are you required to do anything, the answer is no, so you can relax." She started to straighten up her desk. "Janie's parents are doing most of the work. Or I should say Doris is doing the work. Marvin is still off on a trip to the moon on gossamer wings or wherever it is he goes when he gets that For Rent look on his face." She paused for a moment. "God, I hope our genes are stronger than theirs. Anyway, all you have to do is show up and look proud. It should be a piece of cake. And speaking of showing up, is Joyce going to be there?"

"Joyce? Joyce who?" The lines around Harry's mouth deepened just a touch at the mention of his new wife's name. Joyce was the replacement series in the summer reruns of his life. The only problem was, she was always on location.

Maxine noted the tone and the mouth. He was pressing his back teeth together again in a prelude to going into one of his sulks. This could mean only one thing. "I take it she's still in China?"

"China, Hong Kong, New Zealand, Bora Bora, Mars, Jupiter, Uranus . . ." He threw up his hands. "Since we've been married I don't think we've spent more than two weeks in the same city. If I'd known marrying Joyce was going to turn out to be so lonely I'd have stayed married to you."

"Thanks a lot." Maxine finished straightening and, leaning back in her chair, she crossed one short, well-proportioned leg over the other.

Harry sighed. "I just meant that—"

"You just meant that you're horny."

"I am not!" Harry stopped pressing his molars together long enough to defend himself. He didn't want his ex-wife to think that he felt "that way" about his second wife. After all, he had promised to be faithful only unto her until death did them part and it didn't seem that a mere divorce was enough to break a vow he had kept for twenty-five long years—even if he was remarried.

"Well, if you're not you should be. You've only been married a little while. It's natural that you should want to be with her—physically. When we were first married—"

"I don't want to talk about sex," interrupted Harry with what he hoped was a firm and final tone. Sex was a sore subject with him these days. To put it simply, he wasn't getting any.

"Suit yourself. But just let me say that you're the one who's to blame if you're lonely. You're her editor. You keep sending her all over the world and now you're complaining that she's never home." She wagged her finger at him, "Dear Maxine" in full swing. "You've got to make up your mind, Harry. You can't expect her to be an old-fashioned wife and a new-fashioned career woman all at the same time."

Harry looked mildly shocked. His ex-wife was siding with his second wife. He kept tabs on all the talk shows. This wasn't the way it was supposed to be. "Since when did you get to be such a fan of my second wife?"

"Harry, you know I always liked Joyce. It's not her fault you married her. And it's not her fault that she's in China and you're lonely. Just be thankful that you have a wife whose absence makes your heart grow fonder instead of one whose presence makes you think of rye bread."

"Rye bread?"

"Forget it." Maxine waved the subject away. "You wouldn't believe me if I told you. Besides, there is something else I've been meaning to mention to you about the column. You remember last month, the letter about the absentee mother who wanted to give her child back to her ex-husband?"

Harry nodded. "The one where you said it was O.K. because she had her own life to think about and she shouldn't try to raise a child if she didn't want to and—"

"I know what I said."

"We got a lot of letters about that. A lot of women thought that was great advice. A lot—"

"I made it up."

"You what?"

Having told the worst of it, Maxine retraced her steps. "Well I didn't actually make it up—from scratch. I saw it on 'Donahue'. I needed a normal letter for the column. I can't keep printing stuff about cream cheese and men dressing in monkey suits."

"What's wrong with men dressing in tuxedos?"

"I don't mean tuxedos, Harry. I mean real monkey suits. You know, like gorillas, chimpanzees . . ."

"And doing what?"

Maxine shook her head. "Never mind. In your condition it wouldn't do you any good to know."

"I can't believe you'd actually make up a letter."

"From a possible scenario." Maxine retracted her confession just a little further. The fact that so many women had written letters to the editor proved it was an issue that needed her attention, didn't it? And the fact that nobody had actually written her a letter about it was really little more than a technicality.

"I don't know, Maxine." Harry shook his head. "There are ethics. There are rules. As your editor I have to say I'm very disappointed in you. Please don't let it happen again. And as your ex-husband I have to say . . . Tell me what they were doing in those monkey suits. Please."

Maxine breathed a silent sigh of relief. She had expected Harry's standard "journalistic integrity" lecture, but he had let her off easy. "Maybe later." She looked at her watch. It was after five. She stood up. "Well, it was nice talking to you, Harry, but I've got to go."

Harry remained seated. Somewhere in between his office and Maxine's he had begun toying with the idea of asking his ex-wife to have dinner with him. He was fed up with eating alone, and besides, with Bradley getting married on Saturday he was beginning to feel more than a little nostalgic for their marriage. And, he had to admit, he was lonely.

"Harry, I said I have to go." Maxine pointed at his legs, stretched out like a barricade across the only open space in the office.

"What's the rush? I though maybe we could go for a drink. Or have dinner? We could go back to your place. Maybe you could just whip up a little something, you know. You're such a terrific cook."

Maxine shook her head. "Oh, no, you don't. Just because you miss your wife, don't expect me to pinch-hit for her—in any room in the house. Besides, I've got a date."

Harry sat up, alert. "A date? With a man?"

Maxine took her compact out of her purse and checked her face. "That's the usual arrangement."

"Who is he? What does he do? Where did you meet him?" demanded Harry, firing off a staccato barrage of questions like an anxious father whose teenage queen is off on her first date.

Maxine held the lipstick poised just in front of her mouth. "Uh, Harry, I don't know if this has just slipped your mind or what, but you are Bradley's father, not mine, remember?"

"I was just asking."

"And I'm just saying it's none of your business." Maxine applied a fresh coat of lipstick, replaced the tube and the compact in her purse and snapped the clasp shut. Then she noticed the look on Harry's face and decided to relent. "Oh, all right, if you're going to look like that. His name is Solly Berman. He's a doctor and I met him while I was jogging in the park. O.K.?"

Harry bolted to his feet. "You talked to a stranger in the park? Are you out of your mind?" He shouted, all his husbandly proprietary urges surging into action.

"He wasn't a stranger. He was a jogger," corrected his ex-wife.

"A jogger?" cried Harry, flailing his arms in disbelief. "Muggers can be joggers, rapists can be joggers, kidnappers can be joggers! Maxine, this is New York City, for God's sake, every criminal on the streets is running!"

"It wasn't as though he was running with a television set under his arm, Harry."

But Harry was still shaking his head.

She patted down the collar of her blouse. "Solly seems like a nice man. He's a widower. And anyway, we're just having dinner—at his place." As soon as she said it, she regretted adding this last piece of information.

"You're having dinner, with a widower, at his place?" Harry was shaking his head so fast his eyes were having trouble keeping up. "Maxine, you don't know what men are like. You've been married all your life. After dinner he's probably planning on serving dessert in the bedroom!" Harry began pacing in the small office. Two steps up, two steps back.

Maxine looked up into her ex-husband's rapidly reddening face. "And what exactly did you have in mind for after dinner—mints?"

"That's different. You're my—"

"Ex-wife. And if I want to date another man, sleep with another man, go to Timbuktu with another man, then that's precisely what I intend to do. You don't own me, Harry."

Harry paled and swallowed hard. "You mean you'd actually have sex with another man?"

Maxine shrugged. "If I felt like it. But as far as I know, I'm just having dinner with Solly."

A fistful of air forced itself down Harry's nose. "First it's dinner," he snorted. "Then it's breakfast. The next thing you know, you're on your way to Quogue for the weekend."

"Harry, you're jealous?"

Harry lowered his voice. "Jealous? Of course I'm not jealous. Why would I be jealous? I'm just . . . concerned. That's it, concerned. One of my employees is about to put herself in a possibly dangerous situation by having dinner in a strange man's apartment, a man she knows absolutely nothing about. And in this day and age that can be fatal," he cautioned her. "Remember Looking for Mr. Goodbar? Huh? Huh?"

"Solly isn't the type to own a strobe light."

"You think you're so smart. What about Fatal Attraction?"

"Rabbits aren't in season right now."

"You're missing the point!" cried Harry in frustration. "What I'm trying to say is, going out with strangers can be dangerous."

Maxine shook her head. "Oh, Harry, for God's sake. I'm just having dinner with a nice man I met in the park."

But Harry, who had been watching too many late-night news broadcasts while Joyce had been away, had managed to work himself into an absolute frenzy of urban paranoia. "What about the letters you get? Those people are probably jogging in parks all over this country, and people probably think they're 'nice' too, until they expose the seamy underside of their perverted lives to you."

"The seamy underside of their perverted lives?" she quoted back to him, laughing. "They're just trying to cope with life like the rest of us, Harry. Of course some of them cope a little less well than others but . . ." She shrugged. "Have you been eating all right?"

"My diet is not the topic of this discussion!" he cried, slamming his fist into the top of Maxine's desk. It hurt. He paused to let the pain subside and to catch his breath. While he was doing so he had time to consider if maybe he was going just slightly overboard. He decided he was. But the idea of his ex-wife dating had hit him a blow he hadn't been expecting. It was a possibility he had never seriously considered. "It's only natural I should be . . . concerned about you, that's all," he finished off lamely.

Maxine nodded. She understood exactly what was going on. She had had a letter about something very similar only last week. "Well, just to alleviate your natural concern as an employer, maybe you'd like to have a look at this." She picked up a file folder from the desk. The white label on the outside said "Berman, Dr. Solly S."

Harry took the folder. "You had him checked out?"

"We have a research department. I had him researched." She shrugged. "You can read it if it will make you feel any better." She moved past him to the door and then stopped. "Harry, I think it's sweet that you're jealous, but—"

"I told you I was just con—"

"All right, concerned then. But you have to understand that I was 'concerned' about Joyce in the beginning. I felt all the things you're feeling now, possessive, left out, jealous. But I realized that you have your life to live, and I have mine, and we have to put the past behind us. I want to find someone to love, someone to be with, just the way you did. And in the meantime, I'm enjoying my freedom to do exactly as I please with whomever I please. It's the first time in my whole life I've been able to do that."

She took her raincoat from the coat stand and then, looking back over her shoulder, she said, "You'll just have to get used to the idea that you're not the only one who got divorced from our marriage." And then she turned and disappeared down the hallway.

CHAPTER TWO

IT WAS A SMALL, unprepossessing building on East 45th Street. It crouched anonymously between two gray granite monoliths typical of the kind that had been springing up ever since a spate of renovating had struck the area about five years before. As usual, Bradley looked first to his left and then to his right before going through the revolving door into the lobby, just to make sure no one he knew, or no one who knew him, would see him entering the place.

He rode the creaking, shuddering elevator up to the seventh floor and with another furtive glance both ways before getting off, he hurried down the hall to a door boldly marked Suite 709, and then in smaller letters underneath, City Cryo Clinic, and slipped inside.

He nodded self-consciously at the small round Latino woman at the reception desk, and she greeted him with a broad and knowing smile. "*De nuevo*, Mr. Kraft?" Then she winked at him as he walked up to her desk. "That's six times already this week. *Tu estas muy viril, si?*"

Bradley felt the flesh on his face begin to burn. Maria was the motherly type, and her comments always embarrassed him. It made him think of what his own mother would say if she knew what he was doing here, which, thank God, she didn't and never would. But at least Maria was better than Carmelita.

The previous receptionist, who had been behind the desk when he first started to come to Suite 709 nine or ten months before, didn't speak much English either, but she had been young and very pretty in a dark, lush Latino way. Her skin was suffused with a sort of permanent sun-kissed erotic glow, and she smelled faintly of mangos—or was it bananas? Anyway, it was ripe. Not that he had really noticed her, of course. But she had a way of looking at him that said she would like to get to know him—in the biblical sense. That had been enough to make him feel uncomfortable, under the circumstances. But on top of everything else, whenever he would walk past her desk on his way inside, she would flick the succulent pink tip of her tongue suggestively over the juicy roundness of her bottom lip. The implication was obvious and it made him feel all squirmy inside.

Evidently Carmelita's suggestive tongue had made other men feel "all squirmy inside" too—men who did not have Bradley's superior sense of self-control. That of course had been bad for business. Production went up, but inventory went down. It wasn't long before the doctor got wind of what was going on and fired her. Bradley was relieved. He wasn't sure how much longer his superior self-control would have held out. He was glad the first day he had come in and seen Mother Maria sitting behind the desk.

"I'm getting married on Saturday," he said by way of an explanation. "So I won't be around for a while."

Maria nodded understandingly. "*Si. Tu guardas por la novia.*"

Bradley nodded back, "Yes . . . well, I know it's not the usual procedure, but do you think you could have my check ready when I leave?"

"*Si, si, no problema,*" said the receptionist. "I make sure Dr. Carter sign it. He will not mind making an *excepcion* for you. You are practically *familia, si.*"

Bradley thanked her. He glanced over at the door behind her desk and took a couple of sideways steps toward it. "Well . . . ah . . . I guess I'll just go on in, then."

"*Que te diverta!*" chuckled Maria with a devilish grin.

Bradley blushed a little deeper. Maybe he was too conservative, but he didn't think this was any laughing matter. It was just a job and he had to get on with it. He wasn't here to *enjoy* himself, he thought, trying to ignore Maria's wickedly suggestive laugh.

He was almost through the opaque door that led to the private rooms when she called after him. "*Senore* Kraft, we have some new magazines," she teased. He blushed deeper still.

But before he could say anything, if indeed he could have thought of a response to make, another man coming through the door bumped into him. They both apologized, made eye contact and then looked sheepishly away. This was not the sort of place either of them wanted to be seen going into or coming out from. When it came to the celebration of masculine prowess, a sperm bank did not have quite the same elan as a squash club.

By the time Bradley got home, the soft November twilight was beginning to gather over the section of the city they called SOFI, a Manhattanesque abbreviation for a part of the island that in its shabbier days had simply been referred to by its street numbers, but now that it was becoming upmarket apparently required an appellation with more purchase-appeal, because Yuppies didn't live on streets, they resided in *areas*.

A cold breeze was sweeping up the avenues. It carried the oily, salty smell of the harbor, but Bradley took a deep breath anyway to fortify himself before going inside. He was exhausted and he hoped Janie would not be home so that he could crawl into bed and have a little snooze before she arrived.

Lately she had been questioning him about why he was so tired all the time. At first he had told her he just had a bit of a bug, and that had held her off for a while. Especially when he had made a point of coughing and sneezing whenever she was nearby. Then he told her it was just pre-wedding jitters. But, because of his trips to Suite 709, it had been a month since he had last been able to summon up the energy to make love to her, and she was beginning to get both suspicious and annoyed.

But that was all over now, he thought, mounting the steps to the front door. All he needed was a good rest and he would make up to her for lost time. In Aruba. With this last check safely folded in his wallet he had managed to get enough money to pay for a surprise honeymoon. He knew she would be thrilled. He had made such a big deal about her paying for the wedding. Had told her he just couldn't face having her pay for the honeymoon too, so, there would be no honeymoon. She had acquiesced. But he knew how disappointed she had been. Still, she hadn't insisted. Some time ago they had reached an unspoken understanding that her success in the business world was a sore point with him. So she didn't wave her money under his nose. And for that he loved her even more. Enough to do what he had been doing these last few months just so that he could give her the trip she wanted so much.

But he decided not to tell her about it tonight. She would be so happy she would be all over him trying to show him how much she loved him. And he just couldn't take that right now. Of course it was possible that after four long and celibate weeks she might just want to show him how much she loved him anyway. And if she did, he knew what he was going to have to do. He couldn't perform and he certainly couldn't explain. There was only one alternative. An argument. He hoped it wouldn't come to that. He didn't really have the energy.

He hung up his coat in the front hall closet and made his way toward the back of the house. He could hear Janie in the kitchen stirring something on the stove and he resigned himself to putting off his nap at least until after dinner. He yawned as he came up behind her and looked over her shoulder.

"Smells good."

She turned to face him. She wasn't smiling. "Oh, so you're *finally* home." There was a distinct and unmistakable edge to her voice.

"What's that supposed to mean?"

"Nothing." She shrugged and turned back to the stove. But he knew that it was the kind of "nothing" that women say when they really mean "something" but aren't ready to tell you what.

Bradley decided not to push it. "How was your day?" He said too cheerfully, stifling a yawn.

"Obviously not as tiring as yours," she said over her shoulder. There was no mistaking the sarcasm.

"Sorry." He yawned again. "I must have walked twenty blocks. The cold air makes me sleepy."

"In that case, I guess I'll have to start shutting the bedroom window at night."

"What's that supposed to mean?" She was getting closer to telling him what was bugging her and he braced himself.

"*Noth-ing,*" she said tersely and turned off the element under the pot.

Now he knew he was really going to be in for it. Two "nothings" and a scarcely veiled reference to their sex life—or lack of it. Look out!

From the other end of the kitchen came a squawk followed by a whistle. "Chester's hungry," she said to Bradley, pouring the contents of the pan into a small plastic dish. She blew on it for a minute to cool it down a little. "Here, give him this, would you?"

Realizing that the dinner she had been cooking was not for him, Bradley became a trifle irritable. If he couldn't have sleep, he at least wanted to be able to count on having food. "He's your guest, you feed him."

"Pardon me for asking."

"Well, it's disgusting. He keeps barfing all the time."

"He's not *barfing*. He's regurgitating his food. They do that for their mates, and he thinks that I'm his . . . well, you get the idea."

Bradley grimaced at the thought. "Great. I'm about to marry a woman who's been two-timing me with a bird," and he walked out of the kitchen.

He lay down on the couch. He could hear her talking softly to the parrot. "Stupid bird," he muttered to himself. Janie and her animals were beginning to get on his nerves. But then, these days, everything was beginning to get on his nerves. He figured it might be a chemical imbalance brought on by an excess of hormones, which had been brought on by an excess of—well, never mind. But he wasn't sure. In any case, he wasn't about to go to a doctor to find out. He wasn't going to start telling the whole world what he had been doing.

After a few minutes Janie came into the living room. "Are we having a fight?" she asked, sitting on the edge of the couch next to him.

Bradley shook his head. He didn't mind having an argument, but he didn't want to have a fight. Not just before the wedding. "No. I'm sorry I was late. I just went out for . . . a while to get some air." In the kitchen Chester squawked again and flapped his wings. "And to get away from him."

"I'm sorry, he won't be here much longer. Dolly's picking him up Thursday afternoon. I know he's been driving you crazy. But the advertising agency thought that if he was with me—you know, one on one—I might be able to get him to say it right. The client is getting impatient. Chester is their new spokesbird. He's the center of their whole spring campaign. And I'm the only one he'll respond to."

Bradley felt a pang of guilt. She was working hard for the two of them and all he could do was complain. "And why not?" he said, taking her hand in his. "Parrots are supposed to be very intelligent birds."

"Are we making up?" She smiled and leaned over and placed a kiss softly on his lips. At first he kissed her back. But then she slowly began to increase the pressure of her mouth on his. He recognized the signs and slowly he eased her away from him.

She looked puzzled and hurt. "Bradley . . . why don't you want to make love to me anymore?"

This was the moment he had been dreading. What could he say? Not the truth, that was for sure. He decided to take the offensive. He hated to do it, but at least it would cool her off until he was able to show her how much he loved her. "Maybe I don't find the smell of flea powder to be an aphrodisiac."

"That's not very nice!" She wrenched her hand from his.

He realized he'd gone too far and he reached for her again. "Just kidding."

"No, you weren't." She brushed his hand away. "Something's bugging you, isn't it. I mean really bugging you. Is it something to do with the wedding? Have you changed your mind about . . . us? Why won't you—"

But before she could finish, Chester took a sweeping dive through the kitchen door. "Mountain Hartz!" he screamed as he sailed over their heads and landed on the top of the bookcase. "Mountain Hartz!"

"That's what's bugging me. I have to listen to that all bloody day long." Bradley sat up. "No more bringing your work home with you when we're married. I'm going to have to put my foot down."

Janie stood up. "Is that right? Well, you don't seem to mind my bringing my paycheck home, and that"—she pointed to Chester, who was busy digging his toenails into the mahogany—"is part of where it comes from."

Bradley clenched his fists. "You just can't leave it alone, can you? Can't let an evening go by without reminding me which one of us is the breadwinner around here?"

"I'm not *reminding* you. I'm just stating a fact. We agreed when we moved in together that I would work and you would stay home and take care of the house. That's what you wanted. But now you seem to resent it."

"We agreed that you would *work*. We didn't agree that you would become the Charles Lazarus of the pet industry."

She moved away from the couch and then turned around to face him, one hand on each hip. "Oh, so it's not the fact that I bring home the bacon that's bugging you. It's how much bacon I bring home. You've never been able to handle the fact that I'm a success. You can't stand it that I made P.E.T. Inc. into a multimillion-dollar-a-year business. Admit it."

"All right, fine, I will. You're absolutely right. I can't stand it!" Bradley jumped to his feet, a rush of adrenaline providing him with a sudden surge of energy. "I can't stand coming home to an empty house while you're out giving pet parties, or opening pet restaurants and pet spas or thinking up some new pet product to market to the public." He strode out into the kitchen and she followed. "I can't stand going to cook myself a pathetic and lonely little dinner and only finding this!" He threw open two of the kitchen cupboards. All three shelves in both cupboards were stocked with cans of Pet Party Purée, The Gourmet Feast for Yuppie Puppies.

"The Yuppie Puppie food is what paid for this house!" cried Janie defensively.

"There you go again. Rub my nose in it. Or maybe you'd just like to hit me with a rolled-up newspaper!" And with that Bradley stormed out of the kitchen, down the hall and into the bathroom. He slammed the door and locked it. An argument had been his alternative to stave off an unwanted bout of lovemaking. But this had gotten a little out of hand. They had both said a lot of things that they had managed to avoid saying, until now. Maybe he had gone too far.

Janie banged on the door. "Bradley? Come out of there!" She heard the tap go on and then the shower. "Bradley!"

Suddenly the door flew open. Bradley stood there with a towel knotted tightly around his waist. In his right hand he was holding a large blue bottle. "Would it be asking too much for me to find a bottle of Prell, or maybe some Fabergé Organics, or even one of those generically branded shampoos, anything, anything but Snow-Coat?"

"I told you I bought the company. I—" But before she could finish, he slammed the door again and locked it.

"I use it!" She shouted against the sound of the running water.

"Mountain Hartz!" shrieked Chester as he glided down the hallway and landed near her feet.

Half an hour later Janie was lying on the far right side of the big double bed and Bradley was clinging to the left edge. The lights were out, the window was open and the silence was oppressive, broken only infrequently by the rustle of feathers from Chester's perch near the door.

After a few more minutes of this Bradley felt a warm foot insinuating itself next to his and then a hand snuggling up beside his neck.

"I'm sorry," they said in unison and then, "It was my fault."

They both laughed softly in the darkness. Janie moved closer and started to stroke Bradley's neck and then his face.

"Hmm, that feels nice," he murmured sleepily.

She kept on stroking his face, pressing herself full-length against him.

"Hmm . . ."

Her hand dipped around behind his right ear and she gently scratched the line of his hair.

"I'm a human, not hound," whispered Bradley.

"Sorry," she whispered back, and her hand traveled lower.

Silently Bradley cursed himself for complaining. She was getting into very still waters.

Gradually Janie infiltrated her hand down under the waistband of his pajama bottoms, stroking the smooth skin of his belly and then the more heavily pelted area of his upper thighs. In the dark, Bradley stifled a yawn. Her hand moved ever lower, her fingers searching and exploring, intent on reaching their goal. He felt like his moment of truth was just a couple of inches away. And then out of the night came the call that saved him.

"Hartz Mountain," muttered Chester under his wing. "Hartz Mountain."

Janie sat bolt upright, the heel of her palm digging into Bradley's crotch. "Did you hear that? He said it. I heard him. He said 'Hartz Mountain' as clear as anything." She flung back the covers and jumped out of bed. She switched on the light and ran over to the bird. "Good boy, Chester. Good boy!" she said, stroking his viri-descent head.

"Good boy," said Bradley, and then under his breath, "Thank you."

CHAPTER THREE

SOLLY S. BERMAN, M.D., lived on the Upper West Side in a tall, narrow townhouse that breathed elegance from every one of its long, narrow windows. Like its occupant, the building was old, but old in the manner of fine antiques—it had the worn, lived-in look that only comes from years of loving use by the same owner.

It was a plush house in a plush neighborhood, a circumstance that afforded Dr. Berman an equally plush clientele. And as his practice was primarily devoted to treating the urban wealthy, his work focused for the most part on maladies resulting directly from that status, afflictions that owed their existence to an overindulgence in a variety of substances and underindulgence in almost any activity not required to administer them. And since Solly Berman was very good at correcting and controlling the side effects of urban wealth, he had become over the years a very wealthy man himself. In fact, if there had been a "Fortune 500" for doctors, his name would certainly have appeared high up on the list.

Needless to say, Maxine was more than a little impressed when she stepped out of the taxi in front of 133 West 73rd Street. You might be able to hide the full extent of your wealth behind the polyester anonymity of a jogging suit, but real estate was always a dead give-away. Now she knew with certainty that the information the research department had dug up was indeed accurate. Dr. Solly S. Berman was not just an elegant, refined, fadingly handsome man. He was a catch. And even though she had made a point of telling her ex-husband that she wasn't expecting anything other than a pleasant evening from Dr. Berman, if something more permanent were to develop, well, she wouldn't exactly run screaming into the woods.

As she mounted the twelve steps to the front door her pulse quick-ened. Maybe dating again wasn't going to be so bad after all. Visions of romantic champagne-encrusted evenings danced before her eyes. Maybe she would be one of the lucky ones who married "up" the sec-ond time. One of those second wives who had the world laid gratefully at their feet by indulgent older husbands. Why not? It could happen. To a certain degree it had happened to her ex-husband Harry's second wife.

Harry thought that Joyce walked on water—when she was in town. Maxine knew this because whereas she had cooked for him every sin-gle night for twenty-five years, with Joyce he ate out. And, whereas she had washed and ironed and scrubbed the collars of his shirts until her nail polish was ruined, he now sent his shirts out to the laundry. Apparently he even thought it was just a charming idiosyncrasy that Joyce defined iron only as a mineral, not an appliance. Maybe Dr. Solly Berman would be her ticket to that point of view. If getting divorced had taught her one thing, it was that anything was possible.

She rang the bell and finished her personal pep talk while she waited. There was no rule in the book that said you could date only men who earned less than your ex-husband, was there? And so, like any normal divorcee in the same position, she allowed herself to won-der fleetingly what it would be like to be the next Mrs. Dr. Solly S. Berman.

Solly S. Berman answered the door himself. Maxine was a little dis-appointed by this until he explained that tonight was Bartholomew's night off so they would be fending for themselves. Bartholomew? She was impressed anew. Anyone who had someone named Bartholomew working in their house acquired an added measure of interest.

He took her coat and she admired the hallway, the giant gilt mirror with the tiny fat cherubs cavorting in the corners and the obviously expensive Qum carpet that lay in a casual expression of exquisite good taste across the marble-tiled floor.

"Rachel always said a hallway should make a good first impression," he explained as he came and stood beside her. "You look lovely tonight, Maxine." And gently taking her arm, he guided her into the similarly splendiferous living room.

"Rachel was your wife?" asked Maxine, more out of politeness than interest.

He nodded sadly and then asked, "Would you like something to drink?"

Maxine thought for a moment. She wasn't much of a drinker. And even though a gin and tonic with a wedge of lime would have hit the spot right at that moment, she decided that sherry was more appropriate. It went with the decor.

"Sherry would be nice."

"Sweet or dry?" asked Solly, sounding pleased as he went over to a set of sparkling decanters nestled unobtrusively on a tasteful brass and glass trolley.

"Uh, dry please." Maxine smiled and nodded. It didn't really make much difference. She didn't particularly care for sherry, but it sounded cultivated.

He nodded his approval. "Rachel always liked a good dry sherry before dinner. She said it sharpened her appetite. I have a very fine fino, Tio Pepe," he said by way of an explanation.

"Just sherry would be fine," replied Maxine.

Solly gave a little smile and returned with a narrow crystal glass filled to the brim with a pale blond liquid. "*Salut.*"

Maxine took the glass and raised it to her lips. She sipped. It had a delicate crisp taste, but it was so dry that it stung the back of her throat. She gave a little cough and it echoed in the huge silence of the house.

Solly returned and stood beside her, a tumbler of something on ice clutched in one liver-spotted hand. Maxine wondered briefly how old he was. And then decided it didn't matter. As you got older you realized that age was just a way of keeping track of events. When I was eighteen I met Harry. When I was twenty-one we got married. When I was forty I knew it was over. When I was forty-five we got divorced. When I was forty-six I started dating men who were old enough to be—

Solly broke into her thoughts. "You're a very quiet woman, Maxine. I like a woman who can appreciate silence. My Rachel could go for hours without saying a word, days." He cupped her elbow in his hand. "Here, come and sit down on the couch."

Obediently Maxine sat on the couch. It was white brocade with little blue and gold threads running through it. It had been years since she had had to make small talk and so, for want of something better to say, she admired the fabric.

He seemed pleased. "Rachel picked out the fabric." Then he gave a big sigh. "But she never got to see it, I'm afraid. It was still out being recovered when . . ." His voice caught and his eyes misted over. He wiped his index finger below both lids.

"I'm sorry. I didn't mean to . . ." Maxine fumbled words to express her feelings, found none and took a big gulp of sherry to fill the void. It left a trail of cultivated heat all the way down.

He put his hand, still wet with the tears, on hers. "No, no, it's all right. My psychoanalyst says that I have to confront the situation, to talk about Rachel's . . . Rachel's . . . leaving, before I can come to terms with it. I'm really getting much better at confronting her . . . her . . . departure."

Maxine nodded. "I understand," she said with studied solemnity. But secretly she thought he made it sound like Rachel was some kind of a train about to exit its station. A refrain formed in her mind. "*Pardon me boys, is that the Rachel Berman choo-choo?*" She giggled, realized it had been out loud and excused herself. Then she took another sip of her sherry. Somehow the glass had become half empty. She played with the cuticle on her left index finger. She wondered if maybe she should have stayed home and washed her hair instead.

Her eyes wandered around the room. On every table, shelf and niche there were pictures of an elegant, square-jawed woman with dark center-parted hair. A large oil painting of the same woman, in an old-fashioned wedding dress, occupied the entire breadth of the chimney breast. Rachel may have departed, but she hadn't yet left the house. Maxine suppressed another giggle.

"Would you like to see the house?" Solly broke the silence.

"That would be nice," replied Maxine, standing and swaying just a little, clutching the now-empty glass.

"Here, let me get you some more sherry."

"Thank you, but I—" Before she could finish, Solly had taken her glass, refilled it and returned it to her hand. "Drink. It's good for you. I know, I'm a doctor." He smiled.

Visions of Marcus Welby danced in her head. She took another sip and decided that maybe she could develop a taste for sherry after all.

Solly refilled his own glass and then guided her up the stairs to the second floor. He showed her the den, the guest rooms, the bathrooms and then finally they approached the double doors at the end of the hall.

"This," he said, flinging open the doors, "was our room." He moved aside and Maxine politely peered in. It was a very large, very feminine room, almost—she sought around for the right word—old-fashioned.

"Go in, go in," Solly urged, but she hung back. She didn't want to go into the bedroom he had shared with his wife. She had an overwhelming feeling that Rachel might still be there.

But once more Solly took her by the arm and the next thing she knew she was standing in the middle of their bedroom. She looked around. On the dressing table were Rachel's cosmetics, Rachel's hairbrush, Rachel's perfume bottles, all looking as though she had only just put them down. Maxine supposed that behind the doors to the walk-in closet, Rachel's clothes were still hanging just as she had left them. It was eerie. She shivered.

"Are you cold?" Solly, ever the gentleman, offered her a knitted throw. "Rachel made it."

Maxine waved it aside. "No, no, I'm fine. Just a little hungry, I suppose," she said by way of an excuse and took another sip of the sherry.

Solly crossed the bedroom and threw open a door to another, smaller room. "Come and look at this. This was Rachel's sitting room."

Reluctantly, Maxine crossed the room. Solly flicked on the light switch but nothing happened. "Bulb must be gone," he apologized. "But I think there's enough light from the window for you to see."

Maxine glanced inside. What she saw made her scalp tingle. She gasped. "Oh my God!"

Standing on the far side of the room, next to the window, the white lace curtain billowing gently around her long white skirt, was Rachel—and she had no head!

"Who left that damn window open!" cried Solly, leaping across the room to close the window. Maxine clutched the doorframe with one hand and the sherry with the other. Her heart was pounding wildly. She was having trouble breathing.

Solly shut the window and smoothed down the folds of the dress. Then he turned around to see the pale pinched face of Maxine, which was now barely distinguishable from the white molding around the door. "Are you all right?"

"She. . . . she . . ." Maxine gestured helplessly at the figure by the window. Solly understood immediately.

"Maybe I should have warned you. That's Rachel's dress form. She used to like to sew. That's her wedding dress. She made it herself, and after she . . . went away, I put it on the dress form. Just a sentimental old fool, I suppose."

Maxine took a deep breath. "I'm sorry, it's just that it . . . she startled me a little. It was silly of me." She finished lamely, still clutching the doorframe. "I . . . Could we go back downstairs now?"

"Of course, of course," said the solicitous Solly.

As Maxine followed him out of the room, she began to recover her composure and her sense of humor. Harry's urban paranoia had obviously been more catching than she had realized. "Rachel's maiden name wasn't Bates by any chance, was it?" she asked.

He turned around. "No, it was Gershwin. Why?"

"No reason, no reason," said Maxine and proceeded down the hall to the top of the staircase. Solly Berman may have been a catch, but he had no sense of humor.

Once they had returned to the relative normalcy of the living room, Maxine craned her head to catch the scent of cooking. She needed to put a little something in her stomach to keep the sherry company. But all that greeted her was the heavy lemony odor of furniture polish. It evoked memories of something, somewhere, and then she remembered—her uncle Bernie's funeral, when she was twelve. The coffin had been polished heavily with the cloying sweet polish and when she bent over to look at Uncle Bernie for the last time she had had a good whiff of it. Inasmuch as she had adored her uncle Bernie, she had hated the smell of lemons ever since. They always made her think of death. And the way this evening was going, she didn't need any help in that direction.

Solly was talking. "We sat shiva for Rachel right here in this room. I remember it just like—"

But before he could get any further a small brown and black dog came skidding in from the hallway, took a flying leap and landed right on Solly's lap.

"Where have you been, you naughty girl?" he said softly, stroking the tiny head. The dog licked his hand and then looked up into his face, moist brown eyes dancing with pleasure.

"She sleeps like the dead," said Solly to Maxine.

"In this house, what else?" said Maxine, smiling benignly. He scratched the dog's back. "Probably didn't even hear you ring the bell."

Maxine reached out and stroked a tan flank. The presence of a living creature was a welcome relief. "It's a Yorkshire terrier, isn't it?" It was one of two breeds—the other being Lassie—that she could recognize on sight, but she sounded like an aficionado all the same. "My daughter-in-law—or at least she will be my daughter-in-law when she marries my son Bradley on Saturday—is in the pet business.

"Rachel and I had a beautiful wedding," replied Solly, narrowing the conversation again. Then he looked up. "I'm glad you like dogs. My psychoanalyst said that I would benefit from the company of one of these little creatures. You know, to help me deal with my grief and to start relating to other living creatures again, get back into the mainstream of life and put the past behind me."

"I understand pets can be very therapeutic," agreed Maxine, glad of the chance to talk about anything other than Rachel. "What's her name?"

"Rachel," said Solly, and hearing its name the little dog licked his hand again.

Solly looked at his watch. "Dinner should be just about ready." He stood up. "Bring your glass. We can finish our drinks in the kitchen. Come on, Rachel."

Maxine followed him and Rachel junior toward the back of the house and the kitchen, glad of any activity that would take her away from the ubiquitous gaze of the Rachel in the living room.

"I hope you like lemon sole," said Solly.

"Love it," replied Maxine, a frozen smile stretching her lips wider than necessary. She swallowed hard. It would have to be *lemon* sole.

"Good. It's—"

Maxine interrupted. "I know. Don't tell me—you were about to say it was one of Rachel's favorites."

Solly turned and smiled. "No, Rachel couldn't stand lemon sole. It's one of *my* favorites."

"Oh." Maxine felt more than a little foolish then. Maybe she was overreacting. The man had to mourn his wife, after all. She was just being overly critical and overly sensitive. It must be the sherry.

"How long has Rachel been . . . gone?" She asked in atonement.

"Seven years," replied Solly, his back to her as he dished the sole onto the plates. "But it seems like yesterday."

"More like today," muttered Maxine.

Solly put the plates on the table. "You don't mind if we eat in here, do you? It's so much more intimate and less formal than the dining room."

Maxine shook her head. "No, this is fine." There were probably pictures of Rachel in the dining room.

Solly pulled out her chair and she sat down. Then he pulled out the chair at the head of the table and, picking up the Yorkshire terrier, he placed her in the seat. "You don't mind, do you? This was Rachel's chair."

Resignedly, Maxine shook her head. "Mind? Why should I mind?"

Then he took the chair opposite her. "Dig in, as they say," he said, lifting his knife and fork.

Maxine took a bite. It wasn't too bad. At least the fish overpowered the lemon instead of the other way around.

"You know," said Solly, "originally I had thought of having Rachel freeze-dried."

Maxine swallowed a lump of fish and, unable to hide the incredulous tone in her voice, said the obvious. "You mean like coffee?"

"More or less." Solly smiled. "I knew you would understand." He shrugged. "But they wouldn't let me do it. It was too experimental at the time. They didn't know how long she would last."

"She's doing pretty well as it is," said Maxine, who couldn't stop herself at this point.

But Solly, whose mind was busy roaming around in the past, didn't hear what she said. "So I prepared Rachel's body myself, right here on this very table. It was such a moving experience. I can't tell you how much closer it brought me to her, to share that last act of intimacy with her."

Maxine sat for a moment, a morsel of sole poised halfway to her mouth, fumes of lemon and specters of death assaulting her. She waited for the implications to sink in. They did. And suddenly all that dry sherry began to feel very wet in her throat.

Her fork clattered to the plate. "Will you excuse me, please," she said and dashed out into the hallway in search of a bathroom, or failing that, a large potted plant.

An hour later she was home, in bed, her address book clutched firmly in one hand and a red marker in the other. She drew a double line through "Berman, Dr. Solly S." And next to the name she added one word—"Psycho."

CHAPTER FOUR

LUBA, WHOSE NAME HAD BEEN MARIANNE when she had lived in Albany, wore Reeboks and cheered on her high-school football team, had hit Bloomingdale's first, then Barney's, Macy's and finally a couple of counter-culture shops in the Village. The Bête Boîte and Deva Station, which sold army surplus, vintage clothing and discounted Norma Kamali, though not necessarily in that order. By the time she reached Tribeca, another trendy toponym for the wedge of land in the Triangle Below Canal Street, it was dark. But she walked along, happily swinging her shopping bags, impervious to the solitary thunk-thunk of the heels of her army boots on the sidewalk or the desultory and deserted state of the streets.

A block later, when she turned the corner onto Thomas Street, between the black huddle of buildings that was her destination, she caught a glimpse of a narrow rectangle of sky. The new moon was rising, lounging on its back in the navy blue night like a piece of celestial costume jewelry with a broken pin. Luba reached into her pocket. She had no money, but she turned over the American Express card and made a wish, although it was a little redundant because her wish had

OLIVIA DE GROVE

already been granted earlier that afternoon. Then she went inside to
tell Paulie the good news.

In New York, there are lofts and then there are *lofts*. Paulie's loft
occupied the entire second floor of the building at number 8 Thomas
Street and was more like a luxury uptown co-op than a downtown
alternative living space. Even though it was tucked away from prying
eyes inside the deceptively rundown warehouse, it had all the ameni-
ties money could buy and then some, including an intercom system
outside the front door of the building.

Luba leaned close to the speaker and called out. "It's me, Paulie. Let
me in. I forgot my key."

A second later the buzzer sounded and Luba left the dirt and grime
of the outer world for the pristine marble magnificence of a vestibule
that signaled to anyone who was allowed to get this far that the resident of this particular loft was loaded. And Paulie was loaded indeed.
In fact, she was so well-heeled that the only word that described her
appropriately was "heiress".

Pauline McCormick, the slender thirty-six-year-old owner of this
and two other buildings on the street, was the only child of the man
who had started Buddy's Bakeries, later to become McCormick Foods
International. To say that there was never any chance she would go
hungry was therefore an understatement.

Of course Buddy McCormick would have preferred a daughter
who wore dresses instead of pants; who lived in suburbia rather than
*sub*urbia; and who had a husband and three children instead of a syn-
thesizer and three guitars, but, all in all he figured that Paulie wasn't
the worst daughter a man could have, though he didn't invite her out
to the country club too often.

When Luba arrived upstairs she flung her bags down in the hallway and hurried into the dimly lit living room. She was dying to tell
Paulie the news, but she wanted to savor the moment, not just blurt it
out. After all, it wasn't every day a wish came true.

"God! I'm bushed," she cried, flinging herself onto the couch. "I've
been shopping," she added as an afterthought.

Paulie was sitting in the tub chair across from the couch, the heel of
her left foot balancing on her right knee, a guitar resting comfortably

34

on her lap. Behind her on the wall was a large framed poster of her band, Drek, with Paulie in leather jeans and a torn T-shirt standing menacingly in the center, holding her favorite guitar like a machine gun.

"Listen to this." She played a couple of riffs. "What do you think?"

"Hmm." Luba wagged her hand back and forth. "It needs work," she said and then, dismissing the music, "Don't you want to know what I bought?"

"You know clothes don't interest me," replied Paulie, running a hand through her short-cropped black hair.

"Don't you want to know how much I spent?"

Paulie shrugged indifferently. "I'll find out when I get my American Express bill."

Her indifference infuriated the younger girl, and Luba leaped to her feet and grabbed the largest of the bags, which happened to have the Bloomingdale's insignia on it.

"You've just got to see this!" she cried, tugging a tissue-wrapped something out of the bag. "I nearly died when I saw it!" She ripped off the tissue and flung it onto the floor. "Look!" She waved the jacket over her head. "Isn't it gorgeous?"

Paulie raised one heavy black eyebrow.

Undaunted, Luba continued to extol the virtues of her purchase. "It's a pilot's jacket. Just like the ones they used to wear in the war. Not Vietnam. The one before that. Or was it the one before the one before that?" She stopped to think, her young face creasing with the effort. "Oh well, it doesn't matter. The point is, it's an authentic copy of an original flight jacket. See, they even made it from distressed leather so it would look old." She brought the jacket over for Paulie to examine.

Paulie felt the sleeve. "Distressed? It looks more like suicidal to me. What was the pilot—a kamikaze? It's crap."

Luba's face fell. "You don't like it."

Paulie sighed. "It's not that I don't like it. It's just that if you're going to buy leather, buy good leather. This stuff is obviously made from split skins. It's stiff and it'll crack the first time you wear it in the cold."

Luba defended the jacket. "But that's the whole point."

Paulie shrugged.

Luba chewed on her bottom lip for a moment. "O.K., O.K., I'll take it back." Disappointed, she put the jacket back into the bag. She didn't feel like showing off the rest of the things she had bought. Not now. Paulie could be so critical. Then she remembered her news.

"Hey, guess what?"

"You know I don't like to play guessing games." Humming to herself, Paulie strummed a few chords on the guitar.

Luba persisted. She wanted the other woman to tease the news out of her. "Don't you want to know why I went shopping?"

Paulie slipped the guitar down beside her chair. "You don't need a why. You shop the way some people breathe. It's an involuntary physiological response."

Luba pouted.

Paulie relented. "But, since I know that all this is your way of getting around to telling me something that's obviously really thrumming your motor, why don't you just come right out and say it?"

Luba took a deep breath and then let it out. "I got the part."

"What part?" Absently Paulie reached for a cigarette, and holding it between her upper and lower bicuspids she struck a match and lit it, sucking a large measure of smoke down into her lungs.

"What part!" cried Luba, jumping to her feet in frustration. "What part!"

Paulie waved her down. "Take it easy and hold it down, will you. You'll wake up Rogue."

Luba immediately clamped a hand over her mouth. "Sorry, I forgot."

"Yeah," said Paulie with emphasis. "You've been doing that a lot lately."

Chagrined into temporary silence, Luba sat down again and picked distractedly at the nubbles in the couch.

"You don't care about my career," she mumbled, her head down.

"What career?"

Luba's head flew up and she stared Paulie right in the eye, challenging her. "I'm an actress and don't you forget it."

Paulie stared back, a thin wisp of smoke drifting demonically out of each nostril. "You're the one who wanted to forget it. Remember after you did those two movies. What were they called now . . ." She made the pretense of trying to remember. "Oh yes, *Ninja Nuns and the Sisters of Satan* and the sequel, let's see what was that called . . ."

"*Ninja Nurses and the Doctors of Death*," offered Luba quietly.

"That was it. How could I forget. Your *career* seems to have consisted of you playing a human sacrifice and a dead body. Move over, Jane Fonda."

"Everyone has to start somewhere," said Luba defensively. And then, to get her own back, "We don't all have daddy's money to fall back on, you know."

Paulie's face softened a little. Antagonistic by nature, she often drove people to the point where they felt the need to hit back before she let them off the hook. "Yeah, I guess we can't all be the Cookieman's kid, can we?" She gave one of her crooked, incredibly Gary Cooper-like grins.

But Luba wasn't about to let down her guard. She pursed her lips and stared at the floor.

"So come on, then, tell me the news," Paulie prodded her. "What part did you get? Something alive this time, I hope."

Luba looked up again. The anger was washed away by a big grin. "You bet it's alive. I mean *she's* alive. I'm the second female lead. I even have lines and I don't have to die or anything." The excitement shone out of her bright blue eyes.

Paulie nodded. She was still somewhat doubtful. "So, what's the picture called?"

Luba hedged. "Don't let the title put you off. It's going to be a very serious picture. They're talking about getting a couple of biggies for the leads . . ."

"What's it called?" asked Paulie again with quiet determination.

Luba took a deep breath. "*The Witches of Wall Street*."

"Jesus Christ!" murmured Paulie.

"What did you say?"

"I said, that's nice." She feigned a smile. There was no point in shooting the kid down in flames. "When does it start shooting?"

"Next week." Luba jumped up and did a little dance. "Oo-ooo, I can't wait. If this picture is a success I can get my career back on track.

There's no limit to how far I can go. I'm only twenty-four." She ran over to the big mirror that was shaped like Marilyn Monroe's head and occupied the wall between the two large windows. She examined her image for a few moments. "I could even change my hair," she said, tugging at the pink and yellow crest of her Cyndi Lauper do. "I could even dress different. I could look, you know, normal." She turned to face Paulie, who had remained silent throughout this little burst of enthusiasm. "Well, I could."

The older woman measured her words carefully, like a parent talking to an errant teenager. "Kid, you can do anything, be anything you want." She paused. "But you can't be *everything* you want. You've got to decide. It's either one thing or the other."

"What are you saying? Why can't I be everything I want?"

Paulie shook her head. "Life just isn't like that. If you want to be really good at something, do the best you can, then you can only do that one thing. It's like me with my music. It's what I want to do more than anything. And so, it's the *only* thing I do. I don't have a husband. I don't have kids—of my own."

"You're a lesbian, for God's sake!"

"We're talking about choices here, Luba, not sexual preferences. I could have a husband, and kids, and a house in Great Neck, and still be a lesbian, if I wanted to. What I'm trying to tell you is, you have to make choices and you have to make sacrifices for those choices. It's that simple."

Luba played with one of the holes in her mesh panty hose, making it bigger. "You're trying to tell me something, aren't you?"

Paulie sighed. "Okay, let's go back. Remember about a year ago, after your last picture? You were so pissed off with the business you said you never wanted to act again."

The younger girl nodded. "I was fed up with being mauled by second assistant directors. You know how it was. They kept wanting to 'audition' me for the part of the body. I had enough, that's all." She shrugged.

"And that's O.K. A lot of girls like you can't take the bullshit. Underneath the pink hair and the counter-culture clothes, you've got white picket fence written all over you."

"I do not!" Luba stamped her feet on the parquet floor. "I do not! I left all that establishment shit behind me when I came to New York."

Paulie raised her eyebrows. "You may be able to take the girl out of the establishment, but you can't take—"

"Don't give me that!" cried Luba, giving one final stomp.

"Look, don't be so defensive. There's nothing wrong with a white picket fence, if that's what you really are inside. I mean, hell, somebody has to drive the Volvo station wagons in this world." Paulie blew a perfect smoke ring, which hovered mystically over her head for a few brief seconds.

"I'm not a white picket fence. I'm an actress."

Paulie corrected her. "But last year you decided that acting wasn't your true calling and you were going to devote your life to something else. Remember?"

"Lots of women have babies, Paulie. We're not all like you."

Paulie ignored the sting. "I could have a baby if I wanted to. I don't need a man, just a syringe. After all, it worked for you."

Luba sprang to her own defense. "It worked for both of us. You wanted that baby too."

"I wanted the baby because you did." She thought for a moment. "And to be perfectly honest, maybe I wanted you to have it because I kind of liked the idea of us being a regular little nuclear family. But now all of a sudden you want to go back to your *career*. And what am I supposed to do? I don't have any room in my life for a baby and it looks like you don't either." Paulie came over and put her arm around the younger girl's shoulders. "Look, kid, I don't mind what you do. Your life is your life. But you've got to make up your mind. What are you going to do about Rogue?"

Luba looked troubled for a moment, but then her face brightened. "I'll return him."

"What!"

"I'll take him back. I'll find out from the clinic who the father was and I'll give the baby to him."

"Luba," said Paulie patiently, "this is a baby we're talking about here, not a leather jacket. Contrary to your experience, life is not like a department store. There is no Refund and Exchange counter."

"Well, have you got a better suggestion? Somewhere out there Rogue has a father. He's probably a nice normal guy with a nice normal job. He'd probably love to have Rogue. I mean, it's not every day somebody comes along and gives you a baby for free. Right?"

Paulie was still shaking her head.

"Anyway, I really think it's in the best interests of the child." Luba latched on to a line she had read in a women's magazine. It seemed to fit the occasion. "Under the circumstances, Rogue would be better off with his father."

The older woman tried to interrupt, but Luba was firm.

"No, Paulie, don't try and change my mind. I'm taking that baby back."

CHAPTER FIVE

JEFFREY MONDAVI STUCK HIS HEAD around the door of Maxine's office. "How's the best-looking lady in the building?" he grinned, his handsome, slightly Semitic features radiating charm, youthful vitality and barely controlled lust.

Maxine looked up. She had been staring at the mayonnaise letter for the past half hour, still trying to come up with some advice that was conventional yet original, helpful yet noncommittal for the woman whose husband wanted to turn her into a sandwich. It wasn't easy. Not only did she have no idea what to say to alleviate the woman's comestible condition but her mind kept seguing to her own peculiar predicament. To be precise she was still feeling the aftershocks of her first serious attempt at dating in over a quarter of a century. Every now and then she would see in her mind's eye the face of the solicitous Solly, or worse, the dead but not departed Rachel, and each time the whole experience became more and more like something out of a Stephen King novel. Somehow the peculiarities of the husband whose wife was going crazy in Cleveland seemed minor compared to those of Dr. Solly S. Berman et al.

And, now that she had had some time to think about it, she had decided that, psychos notwithstanding, she didn't think she had coped all that well with the situation herself. Pausing only long enough at the container of an accommodating ficus tree to remove the very last smidgen of sherry-soaked sole from her stomach, she had fled into the street without even a polite good-bye. Dating was obviously going to be a lot different now than it was the last time she had tried it, when all you really had to worry about was holding on to your virginity, not your sanity, never mind your dinner. Maybe, she decided, she should write to herself for some advice.

Dear Maxine,

Last night I had dinner with Dr. Strange Love and threw up in one of his jardinieres. I forget. Is this what dating is supposed to be like? Is it just me or have the times changed that much?

Becoming Neurotic in New York

"You look tired," said Jeffrey, leaning against the doorframe, his hands stuffed casually into the pockets of his fashionably pleated trousers. And then he winked knowingly. "Had a heavy date last night, eh?"

Maxine ignored the wink. "Let's just say he was a dead weight. And how did you know I had a date last night?"

Jeffrey shrugged. "Trixie told me. You know Trixie—all ears to all people. And I figure, if you're in a dating mode, you might say yes to me one of these days, so I made it my business to find out who it was with. Guy was a little long in the tooth for you, wasn't he?"

"Actually, it was his memory which was a little on the long side," replied Maxine as the cloying taste of lemons suddenly resurrected itself in her mouth.

"So, why not go out with me?"

"I don't do daycare dates, Jeffrey. Now either tell me what you want or get out of my office." She hoped her voice held the tone she intended—pleasant but firm. After all, his attentions *were* flattering and there was no point biting his head off for paying her the compliment of finding her attractive, but at the same time she had no intention of encouraging him, or anyone else, for some time.

"I'm not in your office. I'm in the hallway." He smiled again, teasing her, and she noticed for the first time that he had a slight gap between his front teeth, like Topol. "And if I told you what I wanted it would curl your hair," he added suggestively, dropping his voice to a more intimate level.

Maxine shook her head in amazement. Young people. "Is everybody under thirty in a permanent state of arousal, or is it just you?"

"Hey, what can I say?" He took his hands out of his pockets and shrugged, palms up. "I take one look at you and—"

"And what?" came a deeper voice from the other side of the wall.

Jeffrey Mondavi jumped. Before he could move from the doorway, Maxine saw a shadow looming over him through the opaque glass wall. In a moment Harry appeared.

"Uh . . . uh . . ." Jeffrey grasped around to finish the sentence. "And I, uh, realize that, uh, if I work hard enough I might . . . might have a column of my own . . . one day?" His voice tapered off. His face had taken on the dusky glow of embarrassment. "Well, gotta go. Time is money." He looked half fearfully, half hopefully at his boss. "Nice suit," he grinned, running a knowing hand along the lapel. And then he was gone.

Maxine waited until he was out of earshot before she let out the laugh. He really was sweet. Too bad he was just a kid.

"What was he doing, asking you to the senior prom?" inquired Harry as he took Jeffrey Mondavi's place on the doorjamb.

"I'm not in the mood, Harry, so before you start let me warn you that I'm experiencing premenopausal symptoms this morning and your life is hanging by a thread."

Harry decided to acquiesce to the hormonal threat and change the subject. "I just stopped by to ask you how your date went with the good Dr. Berman."

Maxine nodded. "It went. Enough said."

Harry got that pleased expression on his face that said *I told you so.* "That bad, eh?"

"How bad or how good it was is none of your business. Now if there's nothing else, I have work to get on with."

But Harry remained where he was. What did she mean, how bad or how *good*? "Actually, I, uh, really came to ask you to lunch."

"Lunch?" Maxine regarded him with suspicion. "The last time we had lunch was the day after Bradley's bar mitzvah, which puts it about a decade and a half ago. Don't tell me it's time again, already?"

He shrugged off the sarcasm. "We are the parents of the groom, after all. I thought a little celebration was in order. But if you're too busy . . ."

Maxine regarded him for a moment, weighing the situation. "I don't know, Harry. All my instincts tell me that you've got something up your sleeve. But maybe as parents of the groom we *should* celebrate a little. Where were you thinking of taking me?"

"The Rainbow Room."

"The Rainbow Room?" That threw her for a minute. The Rainbow Room was their "special place." When they were younger they always went there when there was an occasion to celebrate. And he had remembered. After all this time. "Oh, Harry, we haven't been there in years. What a lovely idea."

Harry shrugged his best "ah gosh" shrug. "What can I say?"

The Rainbow Room, which occupies the sixty-fifth floor of the RCA building, was so old it was new again. Or at least it was on the way to being new again. Gone for the moment were the aubergine silk walls, the little tables for two that perched on the edge of the dance floor, the stars, the glamour, the romance, the furniture. Of course, the tall trademark windows still stretched the floor-to-ceiling views off into infinity just as they always had. And the huge crystal-drop chandeliers still flashed prisms of light from one glass column to the next, filling the room with countless tiny replicas of its namesake. But other than that, everything else had changed.

Maxine looked around her in disbelief. "Very funny, Harry. Very funny." She turned to her ex-husband. "*This* is your idea of lunch at the Rainbow Room?"

Harry held up two hot dogs and two sodas. "This is lunch. And this *is* the Rainbow Room," he said, gesturing at the view and dripping mustard.

Maxine clutched her leather gloves tightly in both hands. "Harry, I don't know if this has escaped your notice, or if you're trying to be funny in that peculiarly slanted way of yours, but this place IS UNDER CONSTRUCTION!" She had to shout the last part of her sentence because less than two feet away a carpenter had started driving screws into dry wall with an automatic drill.

Harry nodded, shouting back. "I KNOW. IT WON'T BE FIN-ISHED"—the carpenter stopped drilling and Harry stopped shout-ing—"for another month yet."

"Then you owe me lunch IN ANOTHER MONTH!" cried Maxine against the sound of the drill.

Harry tried to explain, but Maxine started purposefully toward the bank of elevators.

"Wait!" cried Harry, waving the hot dogs and broadcasting a spray of sauerkraut across the unfinished floor. "Hey, wait a minute." He caught up with her by the elevators.

"Maxine, come on. Where's your sense of adventure?"

"My sense of adventure? I already used up my adventure quota for this month, last night." She punched the DOWN button. It failed to light up. She punched it again.

"Ain't it workin'?" asked a blue-jeaned workman in a hardhat.

"Are the doors opening?"

"Hey, Vinnie," called Hardhat to someone in New Jersey. "What's up wid de elevator?"

"Ain't workin'," replied Vinnie from five feet away.

"Ain't workin', lady."

"Thank you for clearing that up for me," replied Maxine with mea-sured civility. "Now that we have established a diagnosis, do you think we could have a prognosis?"

"Huh?"

"When—do—you—think—it—will—be work—ing?"

"Oh, I get it. Uh . . . They're testing de cables. A half hour, maybe an hour, should be O.K. den."

Reluctantly, Maxine turned to her ex-husband. "Well, I suppose you got your own way again. We're stuck here for the time being and if I didn't know better I'd say you arranged it that way."

Harry looked innocent. "Maxine, would I . . ."

"Did you put ketchup on one of those?"

Harry held out the one in his left hand. "Ketchup, mustard and sauerkraut. Just the way you like it."

Maxine took the food. "Thank you." She looked around. "Do you suppose we can get a table without a reservation?"

Twenty minutes later they were sitting on two up-ended crates, on what would soon be, once again, the famous revolving dance floor, finishing off their sodas.

"Not that I'm trying to be nosy or anything, but do you think you could tell me now just what gave you the idea for coming up here in the first place? I've never been taken prisoner for lunch before," said Maxine, checking her face in her compact and dabbing a fleck of mustard from the corner of her mouth.

Harry looked sheepish. "Well, since you've been such a good sport, I might as well tell you. I decided to do a story on the reopening of the Rainbow Room for the December issue. You know, the whole before-and-after thing with pictures and a history of the old place. It is kind of a landmark."

"So was the Statue of Liberty, but we didn't have lunch on top of the scaffolding." Maxine applied a fresh coat of lipstick.

"Well, the truth is that I assigned the story to Joyce, but she got back late last night from the China trip and she wasn't feeling too good this morning. Picked up some kind of a Beijing bug, I guess. So I thought that I could kind of check it out for her, have lunch with you . . ."

"That explains why *you're* here, but it doesn't explain why *I'm* here. Now, what have you got up your thirty-six-inch sleeve, Harry Kraft?"

Harry reached out and took her tiny, soft hand in his. "Remember when we used to come dancing up here when we were first married?" He squeezed her hand gently and looked deep into her eyes. "You used to wear that yellow dress with the white polka dots and the little black bow in the back."

"You remember that dress?" Maxine was amazed. In all the years they had been married he had never remembered their anniversary, her birthday, or any of the dates, sizes or preferences that women know indicates the continued attention and affection of their mates. But he remembered the yellow dress.

Harry nodded. "Maybe it's because I'm getting older, or because our son is finally getting married, but lately I've been remembering a lot of things."

Maxine, whose memory wasn't nearly so attuned to their former life, probably because she hadn't been practicing as hard as Harry, mused out loud, "I wonder whatever happened to that dress?"

"I wonder whatever happened to—"

But before he could finish, Maxine felt a shudder running through her body, as if some distant and powerful force had her in its grip. It was, yes, there was no other way to describe it, as though the earth had moved! "What was that?"

Harry looked deeper into her eyes. "Did you feel it too?" he murmured.

"You folks O.K.?" called Hardhat from across the room. "Don't worry. It ain't an earthquake. They're just testin' de dance floor. See if it still works."

"I hope it works better than the elevators," replied Maxine as she tried to disengage her hand from Harry's. But he held on and continued his deep searching look into her eyes.

"Shall we?" he whispered in that way that he had that used to really melt her margarita.

Something was happening here that she hadn't counted on and had no idea how to handle. Old feelings were beginning to stir. Safe, familiar feelings from a time before the Solly Bermans and Jeffrey Mondavis of the world had complicated her life. But even though she could feel herself being drawn backward into the haven arms of the well-worn and comfortable Harry, she held back. "Shall we what?"

"See if the dance floor still works."

And before she could protest, Harry pulled her lightly to her feet and guided her out onto the floor. And as the old motor cranked back into service and the floor shuddered and began to turn ever so slowly beneath their feet, he began to sing "Sentimental Journey" softly in her ear.

Maxine closed her eyes. Twenty years ago when Harry used to sing that song to her, right here in the Rainbow Room, she was a young wife, in love, with the whole future ahead of her. Now that future was all in the past. With a sigh she leaned against him and closed her eyes, and he held her tighter still while the two of them drifted around the floor on a cloud of memories.

After a few minutes of dancing and a little familiar stroking in the small of her back, Harry slowed down until they were just marking time in one spot. Gently he reached down and tilted Maxine's chin upward. Then slowly he bowed his head down toward her face and placed his lips gently on hers.

As the fragrance of sauerkraut and mustard assailed his nostrils, he pressed harder and more insistently, the lines of their mouths coming together in a well-worn groove. For a moment Maxine responded, accepting the kiss and returning it. Then, suddenly realizing where she was and who she was with and what year it was, her eyes snapped open almost at the same moment as her teeth clapped shut. "What the hell do you think you're doing!"

Harry's eyes opened, but he held his lips firmly mashed against hers and managed to answer. "Did you sleep with him?"

"*Arrrrghhh!*" replied Maxine, pushing him away at the same moment that the dance floor, with an ominous grinding noise, shimmied to a halt.

"Gonna have to do somethin' about dat motor," said Hardhat to Vinnie.

"So that's what this is all about! All this remembering. All this singing and dancing and sauerkraut and ketchup and . . . and . . . You, you just wanted to know if I slept with another man."

Even though the jig was up, Harry still pressed his point. "I have to know, Maxine. It's been driving me crazy. Did you sleep with him? Was it any good?"

"You're sick, Harry, really sick." She turned and started to walk away from him, her emotions churning in much the same fashion as her stomach had the night before. Men!

"Maxine?" He caught up with her and took hold of her arm.

Taking a deep breath to compose herself, she turned to face him. "Harry, listen to me. I am not your wife anymore. Who I sleep with and who I don't sleep with is none of your business."

Harry hung his head. She was right, of course. But the thought of her being with another man was something he found hard to swallow.

All those years she had been his, only his. Now she was up for grabs, and he couldn't stand the idea. It was like seeing the first car you ever owned—the one you had worked after school and on weekends for two whole years to get—being driven down the street by another kid, a strange kid. It was just too much.

Seeing the look on his face, Maxine softened. Whoever said that divorce was harder on women? "Harry, look, if it makes you feel any better, I didn't sleep with him. It would have been too crowded. But you've got to let go of me, Harry." She said it firmly like a schoolteacher trying to instill a lesson in a reluctant pupil. "We are divorced. It's over between us. You have a new wife and I have a new life. It's time you stopped thinking about the past, about us. I'm not your wife anymore."

"I know that. I know who my wife is. I'm in love with Joyce. I'm married to Joyce. It's just that . . ."

"You can't go through life an emotional bigamist, Harry."

Placed on the defensive, Harry struck back. "Don't flatter yourself. If you think I have any lingering feelings for you or our marriage, you're wrong. I'm glad we got divorced. And I'm very happy being married to Maxine, so there."

"See what I mean?" said Maxine.

CHAPTER SIX

A DOZEN IVORY-COLORED CANDLES FLICKERED in the soft winter twilight, their flames reflecting in the well-buffed sheen of the gray and white marble fireplace and again in the Empire mirror that hung above it. The accumulated glow added a soft halo-like luster to the bunches of pink and white baby's-breath, which, captured in ribbons of white silk, lay casually along the rim of the mantel.

Below, a small scented log crackled cheerfully in the fireplace. And on either side of the hearth, like a pair of blazing parentheses, stood two enormous silver sconces, again with lit candles, which were surrounded at the base by a froth of silver leaves woven with baby's-breath and tiny out-of-season violets. It was a beautiful and tastefully understated setting for an early winter wedding, and Janie was very pleased.

In front of the fireplace and slightly to the left, the groom shifted nervously in his top hat and tails and glanced at the door from time to time as if anticipating the entrance of the bride.

The "father" of the groom, the man who had arranged for the wedding in the first place and who had paid the thousand-dollar fee without even blinking an eye, ran a finger around the neck of his tuxedo shirt in an effort to ease the starchy fabric away from his skin. He was sweating slightly, whether from the heat of the fire or from the stress of the situation was unclear even to him.

But as he waited for the ceremony to begin he realized that he hadn't counted on how much this wedding was going to remind him of his own wedding and what came after. He thought he'd gotten over all that by now, but maybe not. Maybe you never get over events that later lead to disaster. After all, did the survivors of the *Titanic*, the ones who had lost cherished members of their families, ever get over that? Weren't there maritime moments in their later lives when it all came back to them? Times when even the sight of salt water triggered a moment of déjà vu and they thought, "If only I had waited for the next ship"? Or did they all live in the Midwest?

And speaking of next ships, he looked over at the bride's "mother." Lavinia Dodge didn't look bad for a woman in her early forties. In fact she was still one of the best-looking women he had ever seen, dressed or otherwise. Still, his feelings toward her were largely ambivalent. He had a typical case of approach and avoidance whenever he thought of her. Specifically, he liked the approach part but wanted to avoid the commitment. No way was he ready to sail on the S.S. *Lavinia* just yet.

Feeling his glance, Lavinia Dodge looked back and, tossing a cloud of red hair over one shoulder, gave him a knowing smile from beneath the veil of her saucy little cocktail hat. It looked like the bride and groom weren't the only ones who were going to be having a wedding night tonight.

A few moments later, a chord of music pierced the murmur of conversation and those assembled took their seats. Then the soft but powerful strains of the "Wedding March" broke into full peal and suddenly all eyes turned to the door. A second later the bride appeared, her dark eyes obscured by the long white veil that trailed from her ornate silver headpiece.

A soft and collective *aah*! erupted from the guests. And as the bride proceeded down the aisle, the light from the candles glittered off the tiny silver ornaments that adorned the netting of her veil. At first glance these looked like bows, but on closer inspection they turned out instead to be shaped like miniature dog biscuits, a last-minute effort by the bride's "mother," who had sewn them on earlier that afternoon.

Finally, side by side at the altar, the bride and groom eyed each other nervously, the bride trembled slightly, and the nondenominational ceremony began.

"Do you, Tony, take Marilyn to be your mate?" asked Janie with all the solemnity the moment demanded.

In response, Tony licked the end of his nose.

Satisfied, Janie turned to the bride and said, "And do you, Marilyn, take Tony to be your mate?" The bride blinked a shy response beneath her veil.

"Then I now pronounce you to be married," said Janie, and her words were greeted by a round of polite applause from the guests.

But, no matter how subdued, the sudden clapping startled the groom, who then kicked his owner sharply in the diaphragm with his powerful hind legs.

"*Oooofff!*" exclaimed Steve in surprise.

Observing the groom's behavior, the bride began to twist herself fiercely from side to side in an effort to get down.

"Marilyn! Stop that!" cried Lavinia Dodge in dismay. "You'll ruin your veil."

But Marilyn, oblivious to her responsibilities to maintain both her decorum and her veil, managed with one flying leap to eject herself from the arms of her owner, landed with all four feet on the pale mauve Chinese carpet and proceeded hell-bent for leather up the aisle, her veil cascading behind her like a white net waterfall.

The groom, not to be outdone, took only a second longer to reach the floor. And with his top hat now slightly askew, he chased the bride happily down the hall toward the kitchen, yipping sharply with the excitement of the moment.

"Thatta boy, Tony! Go get her," called Steve Curtis, watching his bichon frisé disappear after the Maltese terrier as thirty-two toenails gripped for traction on the polished wooden floors.

Lavinia, looking every bit the overprotective mother, followed the dogs out of the room. "Marilyn! Come back. Come to Mother," she called to no avail.

Steve, who had entered a period of postnuptial aridity, had stopped fussing with his collar and was now ready to appreciate the funny side of things. Janie, on the other hand, wasn't sure whether to laugh or not.

"Sometimes these things happen," she said helplessly. "You just never know how some dogs will react to a wedding."

"Dogs and people too," replied Steve, who started out laughing and ended on a more bitter note. "Of course, my wife waited until we'd been married a while before she decided to run out on me."

"I'm sorry," was all Janie could think of to say.

"Yeah, me too. But what the hell. That's life." Steve shrugged his feigned indifference. "Nice ceremony. Real cute. Just hope it doesn't give the mother of the bride any ideas, eh?" A wide, appealing grin cut a swath of pearly white across his tanned face. Janie decided then that he was good-looking, in a depleted sort of way. Added to that, the temples of his black, swept-back hair were touched with gray, which made him seem more like a man entering his fifties than one in his late thirties. The total effect was that of a man who had suffered for some great cause, although since Janie knew that he had made his money in the construction business she thought that was doubtful.

She smiled back. "I'm glad you liked it. We get a lot of requests for these doggie weddings. In fact, it's become so popular we just can't keep up. Of course I don't usually do them myself anymore, but the woman who was supposed to be here tonight called and said she couldn't make it. And since I make it a policy never to let my customers down, here I am."

"My luck must be changing." Steve Curtis was one of those men who tests his charm on every woman he meets—a habit that had got him into plenty of hot water with his first wife as well as with Lavinia, and he now gave Janie the same appraising look he lavished on every woman under the age of fifty. The one that said, *Hey, baby, I like your superstructure.* Most women usually looked back with a tacit invitation that relayed the message that if that was the case, they wouldn't mind having their premises inspected. But Janie began to blush. Suddenly Steve felt he had just said dirty words to a virgin. He backed off. "I'm not surprised you do a lot of these weddings. Gives people a chance to get together, keeps the dream alive."

Janie frowned. "Keeps the dream alive?"

"Yeah, you know, happily ever after? All that shit. That's what weddings are all about, isn't it?" But he didn't sound as though he believed it.

"I hope so," replied Janie half to herself as she bent down and retrieved her purse.

"Say, you're not leaving, are you?" asked Steve in a moment of spontaneous familiarity. "You've gotta stick around for the reception."

Janie looked at her watch. "I really shouldn't."

"Come on," he coaxed. "You can't come to a wedding and not have a glass of champagne and a piece of cake. Where's your sense of tradition?"

Janie thought for a moment. She really wasn't *that* pushed for time. And it would be rude to marry and run. Besides, there was something about Steve Curtis that said he couldn't take many more rejections, not even small ones. He had the look of an abandoned puppy in his eyes. "All right, I'll stay for the toast to the happy couple."

"Great!" said Steve, suddenly feeling more jubilant than the occasion required. "Now, let me introduce you to some of the guests. Might be able to drum up some more wedding business for you. All these people here got cats or dogs. That's how I met most of them, through their pets." And with that he guided her toward the fifteen or so people who had showed up for Tony and Marilyn's wedding.

An hour later, Janie had had three glasses of champagne and she had become aware of two things. First, the wedding cake had been cut and eaten and she was still there. And second, Lavinia Dodge was looking daggers at her from across the room.

"The mother of the bride keeps glaring at me," she said, looking up at Steve, who was casually draped over the arm of her chair, with one hand resting proprietarily on the back of it and the other cradling a half-empty bottle of Dom Perignon.

He looked over at Lavinia and flashed her a smile. He was enjoying himself and he didn't give a damn if Lavinia was busy sharpening her claws. "I think she would like the floor to open up and for you to fall into the hole," he said with amusement and then chugged back another mouthful of champagne.

54

Janie took another cautious look. "I guess she thinks I'm horning in on her territory. I should have realized you two were having a thing. What with your dogs getting married and all."

Steve shook his head. "Yeah, we're having a thing all right. Only problem is, we're not having the same thing. I'm having a present and she's having delusions of a future." He laughed at that, mostly for his own benefit. "But there's no way I'll ever get married again. Uh-uh. No way." He shook his head a couple more times for emphasis.

"You didn't like being married?" Janie, with her own wedding only two days away, wanted to know how everybody felt about the matrimonial state so she could compare notes and reassure herself that all was going to be well. It wasn't that she had any serious doubts, of course. It was just that Bradley had been acting so bizarre lately. Their relationship seemed to be changing into something new. But what?

"Hey, don't get me wrong," carried on Steve. "I loved being married. Greatest place in the world to be."

Janie relaxed a little. That was good to hear, especially from someone who had been so obviously tempered by the candescence of his own uncoupling.

But Steve hadn't finished yet. "Only trouble was, my wife didn't like being married. Not to me anyway. 'Course, I guess she likes being married to *whatshisname*, all right." He laughed bitterly. "She used the same pen to sign the divorce papers and the new marriage licence, she was in such a hurry to get rid of my name and become Mrs. Whatshisname."

Janie sat up. Things were getting a little too close for comfort. And besides she didn't want to hear any more. She had come here to marry the dogs, not to hear a confession from the father of the groom. "Look, Steve, this is really none of my business. I just came here to do the ceremony and make sure the caterer did a good job." She looked at her watch. "Well, would you look at the time! I really should be going."

But Steve didn't hear her. "Did you know I got two kids? Boy twelve, and a girl eight. She lets me see them every third weekend. Ain't that nice? Every third weekend I get to spend time with two little strangers. Whatshisname even wants to adopt them. He must have a thing about changing the names of members of my family." Champagne and pain were making him morose.

Janie tried again to interrupt. "Ah, Steve . . ."

But Steve hadn't finished yet. "That's why I got Tony. He's my family now. Good old Tony." He took another jolt of champagne. "It's not the same as kids, though. God, I miss my kids."

In spite of her desire not to get involved, Janie felt a great wave of empathy rolling over her. She wanted to say something supportive, something helpful. "Couldn't you get joint custody or something so you could see them more often?"

Steve looked even more depleted. "I tried that. But how can a bachelor living in Manhattan compare with a happily married couple living in Fairfield, Connecticut, with a station wagon and a yard? The judge almost laughed me out of the court." He sighed heavily. "I suppose I could ask for a variance on the court order, but I don't want to put the kids through that again. They've been through enough already."

"You could always get married again and have another family," offered Janie the optimist.

Steve shook his head. "Nope. Just ain't possible. All the good women are already taken. Besides, women these days don't wanna have kids. They wanna have careers—like Lavinia. She thinks that buying fancy clothes for all those rich social types to dazzle each other in is a worthwhile way to spend her life. She thinks that having kids is boring." Through bleary eyes he looked down at Janie. "You wanna have kids?"

"Sure I do. One of these days."

"You wanna marry me?" He was only half kidding.

Janie decided to concentrate on that half. "Sorry, I'm afraid I'm one of the good women who's already taken. Or at least I will be as of Saturday."

"See what I mean?" And he knocked back the last of the champagne.

"What about Lavinia?"

"Lavinia?" Steve took a sideways glance at the voluptuous body in the violet dress. "Maybe one of these days when I get tired of resisting her efforts to get me down the aisle. Who knows? But she's too old to have kids now."

"You could adopt."

Steve shook his head. "It just ain't the same. A man's gotta raise his own flesh and blood, you know what I mean?"

Janie was just about to respond when a few more visual arrows darted her way from across the room. Lavinia Dodge was obviously a cum laude graduate from the if-looks-could-kill school of social graces. Janie decided she had done enough empathizing for one evening. It was time to get back to her own life. Besides, she had never been any good at archery.

She started to rise from the chair, but Steve, who had intercepted a few of the arrows himself, put his hand on her shoulder and pushed her gently back down. "Take it easy. I don't have a Sold sign on me yet. If I want to talk to you, I'll talk to you, and Lavinia can go . . ."

"Lavinia can what?" said Lavinia, who had approached the chair just in time to overhear Steve.

Steve, who had passed tipsy and was well on his way to a serious case of champagneitis, looked up and grinned. "Well well, if it isn't the mother of the bride." He tried to wrap a friendly arm around her waist, but she pushed him away. "Where's the happy couple?"

Lavinia pursed her mouth, thought the better of what she was about to say and answered the question. "The bride is asleep on your chair in the den and the groom is curled up in his basket."

"Well," said Janie, taking the opportunity of Lavinia's intervention as her signal to leave, "I certainly hope you both enjoyed the wedding." And she swiveled her hips sideways out of the chair to avoid coming into any closer contact with Steve and Lavinia. "Thank you for the champagne."

"Hey, wait a minute, I'll walk you to the door," said Steve, lurching off the arm of the chair, still clutching the empty champagne bottle.

Lavinia put a restraining hand on his forearm, but he brushed it off. "I said I'm walking her to the door," he slurred firmly, and Lavinia released her grip and anxiously watched him go.

Having put the champagne bottle down somewhere on the way to the front hall, Steve held out Janie's coat for her.

"Sorry if I bent your ear off tonight. I don't usually drink this much."

Pulling her scarf around her neck, Janie said, "That's O.K. We all need to bend a few ears from time to time. Just think of it as part of the service." She put out her hand. "Well, good night, Steve."

Steve shook her hand. "G'night." He opened the door for her and watched her walk down the hall toward the elevators. He waited until one arrived. And then, just as she was getting on, he called after her, "You sure you're getting married on Saturday?"

"I'm sure," she said, and the doors closed on her smile.

CHAPTER SEVEN

"JOYCE?" Harry tapped lightly on the bathroom door. "Are you all right?"

"Uuuuuuurghhh!" came the moan from within, followed by the sound of retching.

"Can I get you anything?"

There was no reply. Whatever Joyce had picked up in China, she was having a really hard time with it. A moment later he heard the toilet flushing. And a few seconds after that the pale ghost of the former Joyce opened the door and tottered unsteadily into the hallway.

"God, I feel awful," was all she said as she brushed past him and headed straight for the bedroom. Not knowing what else to do, Harry followed. He was worried and he felt helpless. He had no idea how to deal with a sick woman. Maxine had never been sick a day in the twenty-five years they had been married. Or if she had, she had kept it to herself. Thank God.

But ever since Joyce had come back from China she had been like this. And he was fast running out of ideas on how to care for her. He offered Aspirin; she refused. He made chicken soup; she said the *smell* of chicken soup made her want to vomit. He brought her washcloth and her toothbrush into the bedroom so she could clean herself up a bit and feel better, and she complained that her gums bled every time she tried to brush her teeth. All she had done other than that was alternate between bouts of crying and sleeping. And, when he had finally urged her to go to a doctor, she said she was too sick to go to a doctor and begged him to just get the hell out of the apartment and leave her alone to suffer in peace. Which, grateful there was at least *something* he could do, he had done.

Unfortunately, while his absence may have provided some peace for Joyce, it had caused him nothing but aggravation. His little sortie to the Rainbow Room, for instance, had turned out to be a very bad idea. There had been too many ghosts up there in spite of the renovations. He had let himself get carried away and Maxine had ended up calling him an emotional bigamist. And while he didn't think she was right, he wasn't sure she was totally wrong either. In fact, there weren't too many things he was sure about anymore, except that he was confused.

Joyce was lying on the bed with her eyes closed. "I think I'm dying," she groaned as he placed a cold cloth over her fevered forehead.

"Does that mean you don't want to go to the wedding this afternoon?" asked Harry in all seriousness.

Joyce pushed the cloth aside and opened her eyes. "Are you kidding? Do you think I'm actually going to let you go to that wedding without me? Do you think I'm going to let all your relatives and friends think that just because I'm your *second* wife I don't count? That I'm not good enough to go to your son's wedding?"

"I—I—" stuttered Harry, who had not been thinking any of those things.

"Well do you?" she demanded with as much force as she could manage.

"No, Joyce, of course I don't. It's just that you're sick." He knew he had to tread carefully now. Whatever was wrong with Joyce was certainly making her emotionally erratic. She ran the gamut from depressed to despondent to depressed, and he had learned in the few days since she had been home not to antagonize her in any way. Just go along. Agree when possible. Keep silent when not. And above all, don't offer her Chinese food.

"All I meant was, if you *want* to stay home, you can. I don't mind," he finished lamely.

"Over my dead body," said Joyce with determination and pulled the cold cloth back into place over her eyes.

With a sigh, Harry left the bedroom and closed the door. Let her sleep for a while. It was the best thing for her. For him too, he thought glumly and went to find the studs for his tuxedo shirt.

A hundred and fifty guests and eighty-five mink coats had gathered at the Holy Blossom Temple to witness the wedding of Janie and Bradley. But the only thing they had been able to witness so far was the anxious face of the groom and the ever-thinning line of his mother's mouth as she constantly checked her watch.

In the room where the bride was dressed and waiting, propped up against a chair because she didn't want to sit down and risk creasing her dress or losing any of the several thousand seed pearls that decorated it, another mother was looking at another watch. "Why don't we get started?" she cried, fussing with Janie's veil for the twentieth time.

"Mama, stop fussing, you're making me nervous," pleaded Janie for the nineteenth time.

"I'm sorry, I'm sorry." Doris fluttered over to the window and peered out again. But all she could see was the brick wall opposite and the long grungy alleyway that led to the shaft of light where the street began. "I don't see anything," she said, twisting her handkerchief into a knot.

Janie sighed. "Mama, relax, please. For me."

Doris came back to where the bride was standing and rearranged the flounce on the skirt of the wedding dress, being careful of the pearls. Then she stood back and looked at her daughter. "So beautiful. My baby . . ." The handkerchief caught the runnel of tears before it could do any serious damage to her makeup.

"Don't cry, Mama. Please don't cry." Janie sighed in exasperation as she reached out a comforting hand. She didn't know how much more of this she could take. Her mother was driving her crazy.

Doris snuffled back another tumble of tears. "I'm trying not to." She sniffed again. "It's just that my baby is getting m-m-married."

"Mo-ther," warned Janie.

"I'm not crying," said Doris in defense. "It's just that you're getting married and you'll never come home again, sleep in your old room, play with your toys." She waved the damp handkerchief once to punctuate each of her expected losses.

Janie rolled her eyes toward the ceiling. "Mama, I'm twenty-seven years old and I've been living with Bradley for four years already, and before that I was away at college for three."

"College doesn't count. And living with is not the same. There was always the chance you would come home again. Now you won't." The sob stuck halfway up her throat.

"Of course I'll come home again, Mama," said Janie soothingly. "I'll visit you."

"Visit," sniffed Doris. "After twenty-eight years of sacrifice, what's a visit?"

"Mama, I'm only twenty-seven," corrected Janie.

"I'm counting the nine months of morning sickness *and* the twenty-two hours of labor."

Janie sighed loudly. Why did it have to be like this? Why?

Doris decided she had made her point. "So, does a visit include staying for dinner?"

"Of course, Mama." Janie smiled her relief. "How could I go the rest of my life without your cooking?"

Somewhat mollified, Doris looked at her watch again. "I'm going to see what's the problem." And much to Janie's relief she left the room.

Just as Doris came down the hall into the synagogue, the door at the back of the temple opened, ushering in a draft of cold November air and an embarrassed Harry Kraft. The room immediately fell silent. The absence of the father of the groom was no longer meat for discussion.

Maxine, who had been waiting by the last row of pews, was at the door in a flash. "Where the hell have you been?" she hissed, though in the dead silence of the gathering it sounded more like a call to arms.

Harry fidgeted, smiled briefly at the assembled faces and tried to look as though he wasn't really late for his only son's hopefully only wedding.

"Joyce is still sick," he hissed back at his ex-wife.

Maxine looked behind the bulk of her ex-husband for the ailing Joyce and found only a vacant space.

"She's not coming to her own stepson's wedding?"

"Of course she's coming. She just feels a little nauseated. She's outside getting a breath of air."

"Air? We haven't got time for air. You're already forty-five minutes late." Maxine threw up her hands. "The rabbi's getting impatient. He has another wedding at five o'clock. The bride's mother is having conniptions." She nodded toward the recently appeared Doris, who was dabbing away the last of the moisture from her eyes.

Harry summed up the situation right away. There were three women to placate. On fuming, one crying and one vomiting. He decided to go for the best two out of three. "All right, all right, keep your voice down, Maxine. These people are here for a wedding, not a news update on the condition of the bridal party. I'll go and get her." And he went to open the door again.

"Wait!" Maxine opened her purse and shuffled the contents around for a moment. "Here, give her these." She held out a package of soda crackers. "If she's got an upset stomach this will help."

Amazed, Harry took the crackers. "You carry soda crackers in your purse?"

"After twenty-five years you didn't know that?" said Maxine, shaking her head to emphasize the unbelievable extent of his ignorance.

Harry shook his head back. He knew women carried strange things in their purses, but never had he imagined that that included soda crackers.

"That's why we got divorced," said Maxine, nodding her disappointment. "Now hurry up." And she pushed him toward the door.

"Wait!" she cried again.

Harry turned around. "What now?"

"Where's your yarmulke?" she demanded.

"In—my—pocket!" It was all Harry could do to stop from saying "goddamn pocket," but this was, after all, a synagogue so he made the extra effort.

"It's supposed to be on your *head*," cried Maxine, pointing an accusing but well-manicured finger at the top of her ex-husband's pate.

"Don't you think I know that?" glared Harry and went back outside.

Ten minutes later, Joyce was seated at the front of the synagogue, near the chuppah, munching on soda crackers and trying not to look as uncomfortable as she felt as the bride's family and Harry and Maxine's friends and relatives gave her the once-over, two or three times.

Just as she was wondering if she could take another five minutes of being the opening act, the music began and Harry and Maxine started the walk down the aisle, followed by Janie's parents, the lachrymose Doris and her husband, Marvin, who had the uncanny knack of being able to seem absent without really being so. At the back of the procession came Janie in all her matrimonial splendor. Bradley, looking tired but happy, was already waiting under the canopy with the increasingly impatient rabbi.

As Janie joined her husband-to-be under the white velvet chuppah, she smiled at him and then, taking a deep breath, she waited for the rabbi to begin.

He didn't waste any time. "Blessed may you be who come in the name of the Lord . . . We bless you out of the house of the Lord . . ."

Harry stole a sideways glance at Maxine. He wondered if she was remembering too. Another wedding, another synagogue, a long time ago.

The rabbi continued. "May he who is mighty, blessed and great above all, send his abounding blessings to the bridegroom and the bride."

He then began a prayer. Bradley looked over at Janie. She looked so beautiful. So serious. Soon she would be his forever. He smiled slightly. What was she thinking?

Janie heard the words, if not the meaning of the rabbi's prayer. For some reason her mind flashed back to the wedding of Tony and Marilyn or, to be more specific, to the tragic face of Steve Curtis. With an effort she dismissed the puppy-dog eyes—the eyes of the wedded wounded. Then she thought about Harry and Maxine, or more specifically, of their divorce. She made a silent little prayer for her and Bradley to avoid either scenario in their own marriage.

The blessing of the betrothal was next. The rabbi presented the cup of wine first to the bridegroom and then to the bride. After they had both taken a sip from the cup he began the address to the groom.

"Do you, Bradley, take Janie to be your lawful wedded wife, to love, to honor and to cherish?"

Bradley looked first at Janie and then at the rabbi. "I do," he answered boldly.

The rabbi turned to Janie. "Do you, Janie, take Bradley to be your lawful wedded husband, to love, to honor, to cherish?"

"I do," replied Janie softly.

The rabbi took the ring. "Then do you, Bradley, put this ring upon the finger of your bride and say to her: Be thou consecrated unto me, as my wife, by this ring, according to the Law of Moses and of Israel."

Bradley took the plain gold band and took hold of Janie's right hand. Just then, a commotion at the rear of the synagogue distracted him. The door had opened and one of the ushers was trying to keep someone from entering.

Bradley heard him say, "I told you, all the gifts are supposed to be delivered to the home of the bride's mother."

Still determined, the interloper pushed against the door again and said something Bradley couldn't quite hear. He looked over at Janie and gave a slight shrug.

By now everyone in the synagogue had turned their attention from what was happening under the chuppah to what was happening under the portal. A low buzz of whispering passed over the crowd like a transient swarm of bees.

Maxine gave Harry a dig in the ribs. "What's happening?" she whispered.

"How the hell do I know?" he whispered back.

"Is something wrong?" asked Doris, apprehensively clutching her handkerchief. The fact that she didn't want her daughter to get married didn't mean she didn't want her to get *married*.

Suddenly, the usher lost his battle with the door and it flew open, revealing a young girl with a cockscomb of pink hair, a red plaid taffeta balloon skirt, black fishnet stockings, army boots and a leather pilot's jacket with a skull and crossbones stitched on the right sleeve. She was carrying a Bloomingdale's shopping bag.

A hundred and fifty people made one collective gasp. Most of them had never seen anyone like this before, especially not in a synagogue.

Doris clutched Marvin's arm. "Oh my God! Do you think it's a bomb?" she cried, pointing at the bag.

Marvin, who had been busy practicing his absence, patted his wife's hand in an automatic gesture of consolation. "Don't be silly, dear. They don't sell bombs at Bloomingdale's" he said vacantly and then went back to wherever he had been.

Once more the intruder thrust the bag at the usher, who refused to accept it. "I told you, you can't bring that in here now. All the gifts are supposed to be delivered to the bride's mother's—"

Before he could finish the girl put the bag down. "This one's already been *delivered*," she said with a giggle. And with a smile and a wave at the crowd she left, closing the door behind her.

"Well I never," said Doris.

"Probably not," said Harry before he could stop himself. And then he turned to Bradley. "Friend of *yours*, I suppose."

"Dad, honestly I don't know . . ."

Just at that point the bag let out a wail that stunned the entire congregation into shocked silence. The usher, who was closest to the source of the scream, recoiled in fear for a moment before getting hold of himself. The he leaned over and did the obvious thing. He removed the layer of tissue that covered the top of the bag. What he saw made him loosen the grip he had so recently gained on himself.

He looked up the aisle toward the chuppah. "It's a baby," he said into the anticipatory silence.

"A baby what?" called Maxine, who was the only one who seemed to be able to form the ability to commit her thoughts to words at that point.

In answer to her question, the usher picked up the bag and hurried up the aisle. Necks craned from pews on both sides to see just what kind of a baby it was.

Realizing that Maxine had taken charge, or had simply had charge thrust upon her by the inability of the others to coordinate any sort of action of their own, the usher shoved the bag into her arms. "A *baby* baby," he said to complete his explanation.

Maxine took a look in the bag and then looked up. "He's right," she said to Harry, who was now peering over her shoulder. "And there seems to be some kind of a note attached to it."

Having retrieved the note, Maxine handed the bag with the baby in it to Harry, who looked around helplessly for a moment. He thought about handing the bag to Doris, realized she didn't look too steady on her feet and then walked over to the first pew and gave it to Joyce.

"Harry, I don't feel very well," she said, clutching the bag as he thrust it toward her.

"Who does?" said Harry and went back to read the note over Maxine's shoulder.

Dear Barry Kraft, it read.

The people at the sperm bank told me that you are the father of my baby, or I guess I should say our baby. I can't look after him anymore and so I decided he should be with you. His name is Rogue.

P.S. I didn't know where you lived but when I saw the wedding announcement in the Times *I thought this would be a good way to get the baby to you. Look after him. Have a nice wedding*

The Mother of the baby

By the time she had finished the note Maxine realized that everyone else under the chuppah was also looking over her shoulder, so at least she didn't have to wait while the note was passed around before she reacted.

"Well," she said, folding the note in half. "She obviously has the wrong man." She turned to her son, who was swallowing hard and looking pale. "Don't worry, Bradley, we'll just find this Barry Kraft and have him face his responsibilities."

Janie signed with relief. Doris choked back a few more tears. And Harry looked over at Joyce, who had extracted Rogue from the bag and was holding him in the same way that one holds a wet puppy—as far away from one's person as one's arms will permit.

"Can we get on with the wedding now?" interrupted the rabbi.

"Of course," said Maxine, and she returned to her spot under the chuppah.

"Uh . . ." said Bradley.

"Uh, what?" said Janie, who had a sudden sinking feeling.

"Can I talk to you for a minute?" asked Bradley, moving closer so that he could whisper in her ear and in the course of that, stepping on her white satin foot.

"Ouch!" cried the bride.

"Sorry," replied the groom and waited as Janie moved her veil aside to permit him access to the ear.

His breath tickled her and she shivered, though the shiver was probably as much from the shock of what he was saying as from the feathering of his warm breath on her skin.

"You what?" the assembled heard her say. "For how long?" They all leaned forward a bit in their seats. "But why?" They craned their necks to hear the explanation.

Janie pulled away from Bradley. "How could you!" was all she said as she flung her bridal bouquet at his feet and, gathering up her skirts, marched down the aisle, staring straight ahead.

Heaving a deep sigh of resignation, Maxine once again took charge of the moment. She turned to her son. "Does this mean that I am the grandmother of a child named"—she tried to swallow the word but it came out anyway—"Rogue?"

Bradley nodded guiltily.

"I see," was all Maxine said. And then, looking over at the baby, she spoke to her ex-husband. "Harry, I think you'd better go and pick up your grandchild. Your wife looks like she's going to be sick again."

PART TWO

Yes Sir,
That's My Baby

CHAPTER EIGHT

ONE WEEK LATER...

Maxine had no sooner lowered the gurgling pinkness of Rogue Kraft into the bath than she heard a knock at the front door, a little furtive at first, but then stronger.

"Just a minute," she called, scooping up the wet, slippery body in a towel.

Reacting to the swift change of milieu, Rogue gave a little chortle of pleasure.

"You think this is some kind of game, don't you?" she muttered against the side of his silky dark head as she laid him on her shoulder. In response he spit up on her neck and a warm trickle of milk and saliva oozed beneath the collar of her blouse.

With a sigh she headed to the door. "I think I've forgotten more about babies than I ever knew," she commented to her reflection in the hall mirror as she passed it, still trying to wipe the warm sticky trail from her neck and hold the cooing, kicking baby at the same time.

"Who is it?" she called as she approached the door with typical urban caution.

"Me."

"Me who?" she sighed with exasperation as she threw the chain lock and the safety bolt. She knew who it was. The voice was indelibly etched in her memory.

"Hello, Harry," she said, opening the door. Then, moving the baby to the other shoulder, she wiped another runnel of dribble from the rosebud lips. "What are you doing here?"

Harry, looking uncomfortable, stood shifting his weight from one foot to the other out in the hall. "Hi." He half smiled. This was the first time he had been back to his old apartment since the divorce and he wasn't sure of the protocol.

"Well don't just stand there. I've got a wet baby in my arms," said Maxine, and then she turned around and went back down the hall toward the bathroom.

Harry took this as an invitation to come in and, after locking the door behind him, he followed his ex-wife down the hall. By the time he got to the bathroom she was on her knees, bending over the tub and trying to hold the baby and wash it at the same time.

"Where's Bradley?" asked Harry with the best of intentions.

"Bradley? You mean the father of the year?" Maxine shook her head in disgust. "He went to see Janie. Not that it will do him any good. There are some things you can explain and some things you can overlook. This is not one of them." She squirted some baby shampoo onto Rogue's head and began to lather it in.

Getting into the mood of the bath once more, Rogue began kicking his tiny chubby feet in the water, sending a soapy spray in every direction. One particularly well-aimed splash caught Maxine right in the eye. She blinked away the soap and the tears that followed.

"I'm too old for this," she muttered, sluicing a container of clean water over Rogue's head. He sputtered and his face started to turn red. But before he could let out the wail that he planned Maxine attacked his face with a washcloth. He kicked with all the pent-up baby anger he could muster and broadcast another shower of water over the front of Maxine's blouse.

"Can I help?" offered Harry helplessly.

Maxine made a half turn. "You never did before." It was an accusation, not a statement.

Harry took the hint. Why Maxine wanted to drag up the past now he wasn't sure. But he knew instinctively that the fact that he had never bathed Bradley was listed on the debit side in the unconscious tally Maxine was no doubt still taking of their marriage. And to offer now to help with the bathing of Bradley's son would not redeem him. Tactfully he retreated to the bedroom.

A few minutes later Maxine appeared, carrying her baby bundle, her blouse more or less soaked through. "Here, hold this," she said, thrusting the baby at Harry.

Harry automatically received the bundle. He hadn't held a baby in over a quarter of a century and it took him a minute to settle the child in the appropriate orientation—face up.

While he did so Maxine stripped off her soggy blouse, and dropping it on the bedroom floor, she walked across to her closet to get something dry to put on. It took them both a moment before they realized that she was half naked except for her bra and that this automatic gesture of intimacy that would have gone totally unnoticed during any one of the previous twenty-five years was now suddenly the focus of both their attentions.

Harry, still clutching the baby as he watched Maxine walk across to the closet, felt a pang of embarrassment combined with a proprietary feeling of familiar interest. Watching one's wife undress was, he had always felt, one of the great benefits of being married. It was how he imagined Ben Cartwright must have felt when he looked out across the Ponderosa. A feeling of ultimate possession with No Trespassing signs all around it. Except of course that his No Trespassing signs were now supposed to be erected around Joyce. He cleared his throat.

Maxine quickly pulled another blouse from its hanger and, with her back to Harry, slipped it on and did up the buttons.

When she turned around she took a clean towel from a pile on the chair in front of the dressing table and laid it on the bed. "Here," she said, reaching out, "give it to me."

"It has a name," said Harry, handing the baby to her.

"Rogue is not a name. It is a political statement imposed by someone with pink hair." While she spoke, and with a little deft maneuvering, she managed to lay the baby on the dry towel and toss the wet towel onto the floor next to the blouse. Reveling in the sudden freedom, Rogue cooed and kicked his feet one at a time and then both together.

"Pass me the baby powder," ordered Maxine, and Harry, quickly scanning the objects on the bed, managed to pick out the right container on the first try.

She sprinkled some on one hand and then, putting the container down, she clutched his ankles between the thumb and first two fingers of her free hand and lifted both his legs together. Harry watched fascinated. How did women know how to do all this? With his legs thus suspended and his shoulders still resting on the bed, Rogue received a healthy dusting of baby powder around his bottom. Maxine then laid him down again.

"Get me a diaper, will you," said Maxine, waving toward the closet door.

Harry went to the closet and after fishing around for a minute or two came back with a tea towel he had found in a red plastic laundry basket. "I couldn't find any diapers and what's that laundry basket doing in the closet?"

"The laundry basket is his bed until I have time to get him a crib and that is a tea towel, not a diaper." Maxine gave him a look that said she had always suspected he was an inept father. And with a sigh of exasperation she went to get the diaper herself.

She returned a moment later. "This is a diaper," she said, waving the bulging paper panty under Harry's nose.

Harry defended himself. "I was looking for the other kind, like Bradley used to wear."

"I never diapered Bradley in a tea towel." Maxine worked the paper padding under the baby's bottom.

"Did I know?"

"You were his father."

"And Iacocca is the chairman of Chrysler. It doesn't mean he knows how to service a car."

"No, he probably gets his mother to do it for him." She turned the little body on the bed and was just about to work the thick part of the diaper up between his legs when Harry stopped her.

"Wait!" he cried. Harry was looking at the baby. He shook his head and moved in for a closer inspection.

"Are you sure that's Bradley's child?"

Maxine stopped fiddling with the diaper tabs. "You think I do this for strangers?"

"It doesn't look like him."

Maxine took a long look at the baby. Harry was right. "So, maybe it looks like the mother." She shrugged. All babies looked like a cross between Winston Churchill and Barney Rubble at this age.

"No, I don't mean that way." Harry waved in the direction of the open diaper. "I mean that."

Maxine took another look. "Oh, that. From what I saw of the mother she was more likely to hang an earring from it than to cut it off."

"Don't you think you should talk to Bradley about it?" Harry said seriously.

"Harry, this past week has not exactly been full of moments for discussing circumcision. You son has been lying on his bed looking at the ceiling like a lovesick puppy—you should excuse the frame of reference. I've had Doris on the telephone at work, at home, and I'm sure if she could manage it she'd call me in the subway and in the elevator. She wants me to do something. As if there was anything I could do. Then, I've still got a job to do. You remember my job? I got a ton of mail this week and it all has to be read and sorted out for next month's column. Plus I have to look after this"—she pointed at the baby—"because our son seems to have no idea how to and no desire to learn." She stopped to catch her breath. "And furthermore—"

Harry held up a hand. "O.K., O.K., I'm sorry I asked."

"And I'm sorry we didn't have a daughter." She sounded weary.

"I know, I know." Harry made a couple of comforting pats on her shoulder.

"No, you don't," said Maxine flatly. "I thought I was finished with all this. That I could get on with my life. I'm not ready to be a single grandmother!" Her voice went up a decibel or two.

At the sound of a raised voice, or maybe because he wasn't getting any attention, Rogue Kraft let out a wail that would shatter glass. Instantly both sets of eyes were on him.

"He wants his bottle," said Maxine with the authority that only knowledge can bring. And she finished fastening the diaper, wrapped him in a blanket and headed toward the kitchen.

Naturally Harry followed. And a few minutes later they were both sitting on the couch in the living room as Rogue greedily consumed his fifth bottle of the day, nestled against Maxine's left breast and tightly clutching the finger that Harry had so foolishly introduced into his left fist.

"My arm's got pins and needles," whispered Harry, easing his finger away. But Rogue was not about to give it up. He stopped sucking and opened his eyes.

"He's going to start crying," warned Maxine. And he did.

Instantly Harry thrust his finger back into the tiny fist and the baby settled down to a bout of contented sucking.

"So tell me," said Maxine, "what are you doing here tonight anyway?"

"I—that is—Joyce has a doctor's appointment just around the corner and I thought that while I was waiting for her I might as well come over and see how you're doing."

Maxine nodded. "Well, now that you've seen how I'm doing, have you got any suggestions about how I can stop doing it?"

Harry sighed. "I'm sorry this happened, Maxine. I told you, Bradley could have moved in with me, but he wanted to come home after Janie threw him out. I guess he wanted to be near his mother."

"Be near his mother! You mean he wanted to be near a babysitter," snorted Maxine. "But I suppose it's better off with me. You and Lois Lane don't know the first thing about babies."

Harry thought for a moment. She was right. Neither he nor Joyce had any room in their lives, let alone their apartment, for children, never mind two generations' worth of children. It wasn't fair, but Maxine had been the obvious and only choice. Still, he felt he had to say something. "I'll talk to him." Although he had no idea what he would say.

Maxine felt she had made her point, and for a few moments a comfortable silence descended over the room, broken only now and then by the sounds of sucking and the odd sigh of contentment from Harry.

After a time Harry broke the silence. "You know something? This kinda reminds me of the old days."

"What?" said Maxine, whose thoughts had been busy running forward, not backward.

"You know, when you and I used to sit here with Bradley." Harry sighed wistfully. "They were good days, good days. There are times when I really miss being part of a family."

Maxine picked up the signals immediately. Nostalgia was about to rear its sentimental head again. "Don't start with the past again, Harry. I've got enough to deal with as it is. I don't need you resurrecting the ghost of our marriage. Is that clear?"

"All I said was—" But before Harry could come to his own defense the telephone rang. "I'll get it." He started to get up.

"No, I'll get it," said Maxine, handing him the baby and the bottle. "It's probably for me. After all, I'm the one who lives here."

Harry took the hint and the baby and got comfortable. He heard Maxine say "Hello" and then "What're you doing calling me at home?" Maybe it was Dr. Berman.

Maxine listened to the caller and then said, "I see. Look, we've already talked about that before." And then another pause. "Jeffrey, please, I've got enough to cope with at the . . ."

Harry stiffened. Jeffrey? Not Jeffrey Mondavi, that little runt from advertising. But his sudden movement dislodged the nipple and Rogue screamed.

Harry hastily shoved the nipple back into the baby's mouth. He didn't want to miss what was being said.

"Just dinner?" said Maxine into the receiver. "Well . . ."

Harry took advantage of the pause. "Maxine, dear, could you come here a moment, please?"

"Just a minute," said Maxine, putting one hand over the receiver. "What is it?" she called.

"I think your grandson needs you."

The emphasis and the implication did not escape Maxine. The course of action was clear. Instantly she saw a way in which she could quite easily kill two birds with one stone. Get the salivating Jeffrey off her back once and for all and shock Harry out of the idea that somehow, their divorce notwithstanding, she was still his wife. Though the Dr. Berman incident hadn't been terribly effective on that issue because of the way it had backfired—and in fact the only effect her disastrous date had had on Harry was to make him more jealous and protective—perhaps a date with someone closer to home, someone younger, someone normal would do the trick.

"I'd love to have dinner with you, Jeffrey," she said a little louder than necessary to make sure Harry got every word. "Yes, next Wednesday would be fine." And satisfied that her decision was going to ease her that much farther down her road to a new life, she hung up the receiver and returned to the living room.

"That was Jeffrey Mondavi," she volunteered unnecessarily.

Her admission was greeted by a stony look from Harry.

"We're going out for dinner."

Harry said, "The bottle's empty."

Maxine nodded. "Time for a burp." And she reached for the baby.

Just as she was rubbing the center of the tiny back, however, there was another knock at the door.

"Now what?" said Maxine, sounding annoyed and waiting for Harry to say "I'll get it." But he didn't. So, still rubbing the baby's back, she went down the hall to the door, threw the locks without bothering to ask who was there and was surprised to see who was standing unsteadily in the hall.

"Joyce!" It was both an exclamation and a question. "You look awful. What did the doctor say?" And all the time she was talking she was rubbing the baby and herding the pale and tottering Joyce into the apartment.

"Joyce!" said Harry, leaping to his feet. He was both surprised and guilty. He had forgotten all about her.

Maxine guided her unsteady visitor to a chair. "Here, sit. Sit before you fall down. Can I get you some tea? A glass of water?"

Joyce weakly waved the offer aside and gratefully sank into the chair. She looked at Harry. "I waited for you at the doctor's office," she said accusingly, though without much energy.

"I'm sorry, honey, time just slipped by." His lips curved up into a sheepish grin. "We were . . . ah . . . just looking after the baby." Harry looked at his ex-wife for confirmation.

Maxine raised a circumspect eyebrow that said "we who?".

"Good," Joyce said, taking a deep breath. "You're going to need the practice."

Harry's brow furrowed into a questioning "why?" Somehow, though his brain had already processed the question and retrieved the answer, he knew why. Oh brother, did he know why! And the knowledge gripped him like a vise as it began to sink in.

"Congratulate me," said Joyce as one big fat tear slid down her cheek and did a swan dive off the end of her chin. "I'm pregnant."

CHAPTER NINE

"OH, SHUT UP!" Janie snapped at Chester, who was singing the refrain from "Blue Moon" as she waited impatiently for the coffee maker to do its job.

Offended by this sudden outburst of verbal aggression, Chester flapped his wings, and then, in an effort to dissemble, he reached around and scratched behind one feathered ear with his longest toenail.

For the next few moments the only sound was the muffled gurgle of the coffee machine. "Why does it always take so long?" demanded Janie, glaring at the empty pot.

Finally the dark stream of steaming liquid began to descend, filling the kitchen with the kind of deep nutty aroma that would bring joy to the heart of Juan Valdez. Satisfied for the moment, Janie turned her attention to retrieving two mugs from the cupboard and cream from the refrigerator.

Chester, shaken from his enforced torpor by this sudden burst of activity, took it as a signal that all was forgiven and began to croon again. "*Blue mooooon, you saw me . . .*"

Janie grabbed a peanut from a bowl on the counter and threw it at him. He ducked as it sailed past his head, and then he watched where it landed. A moment later he dove off the perch to retrieve it. As far as he was concerned, he could sing all night long if there were peanuts being offered.

"Why did you have to teach him *that* song," said Janie to Dolly as she brought two mugs of coffee over to the kitchen table and sat down.

Dolly looked up from the copy of *Rolling Stone* that she had been reading. "I told you. I didn't *teach* him the song. We were laying some soundtrack and I had him in the studio with me. I guess he just picked it up. Besides, you didn't tell me to censor his auditory input when you asked me to babysit for him until you and Don Juan got over your wedding."

Janie pulled a face and poured some cream into her coffee. "Please don't remind me. I still can't believe it happened to me." A week had done little to soften the blow of the chaos on what should have been her wedding day. "Men! I mean you live with them. You sleep with them. You plan a life with them. You think you know them." She threw her hands up in a gesture of despair and confusion. "How could I have been so wrong about Bradley?"

Dolly shrugged and spooned a couple of hundred calories' worth of demerara into her coffee. She had been wrong about every guy she had ever known. To her it was the normal state of affairs. "Personally I never understood what you saw in him anyway. I mean he was cute, but . . ."

Janie stared glumly into her cup. He *was* cute, wasn't he? But it was more than physical attraction. I liked him—as a person. How many men can you say that about these days?"

Dolly nodded in agreement and blew on her coffee to cool it down a little. "True, true."

Chester, restored once more to his perch, took the break in the conversation as his cue to serenade his audience one more time. "*Blue moon*," he began tentatively.

Janie threw a warning look in his direction. "One more time, Chester, and you are going to end up plucked, stuffed and surrounded by cranberry sauce."

Chester hesitated, eyed the dish of peanuts, paused and then decided that now was probably a good time to sharpen his beak. He turned his back to the two women and reached for the piece of cuttlebone.

"Do you want me to take him back with me?" asked Dolly.

"No, it's all right. At least he gives me someone to talk to." Janie sipped her coffee. "You know the worst thing about being single?"

Dolly shook her head. She had a few hundred ideas on that subject but decided that now was probably not the time to list them.

"It's the silence," said Janie. "Without Bradley, this house is full of silence. I can hear it, pressing in on me, driving me crazy." She put both hands over her ears in an effort to shut out the silence.

"I just leave the TV on," said Dolly, "even when I go to sleep. There's always some man talking about something. It's kind of like having a pajama party, you know, except that everyone's wearing suits." She finished her coffee and put the mug back on the table.

"You want me to make some more coffee?" asked Janie.

"No, that's O.K. I've got an early session in the morning. We're laying track for some sci-fi flick. I think it's called *Voyage to the Moon* or something like that."

Hearing his cue, Chester looked up from the cuttlebone. "*Blue . . .*" he began hopefully, but one look from Janie said his beak wasn't sharp enough yet.

Dolly stood up and stretched. "Thanks for the coffee. Any time you want to talk about life, love and the pursuit of Bradley, you know my number. And like I said, if you get tired of Bobby Vinton over there I'll be glad to birdsit for you again."

Janie walked her to the front door. Chester followed a few moments later, swooping down the hallway like a B-19 going in for a strafing run. He landed on the hall table, nearly knocking over the vase of winter flowers that rested there. Janie gave him a dirty look. "Thanks, but right now I need company, even the feathered kind. And who knows, one of these days maybe I'll actually be able to teach him to say something *I* want him to say."

Dolly laughed. "You mean something like 'Bradley is a shithead?'"

Janie grinned. "I was thinking more along the lines of 'Hello' and 'Good-bye,' but you have a point." She opened the door to let Dolly out. There stood Bradley with one hand poised to knock.

"Well, looks like I picked the right time to say adios," said Dolly, slipping past him and turning to raise her shoulders at Janie.

"No, wait!" cried Janie. But it was too late. Dolly was already down the steps and on her way up the street.

Bradley cleared his throat. "Hi," he said awkwardly.

"What do *you* want?" asked Janie tersely, still clutching the doorknob and half decided to slam the door in his face.

"I wanted . . . uh . . . that is, can I come in? I think we should talk." He made a move to take a step forward.

But Janie stopped him in mid-step. "Isn't it a little late for talking?"

"Please." It sounded almost like begging, which is what it was. And it had the desired effect. Janie let go of the doorknob and moved back a few steps into the hall. Quickly Bradley joined her before she changed her mind.

"I—" He reached out to touch her, but she shrugged off his hand.

"You wanted to talk, so talk," she said, folding her arms across her chest.

Realizing he would have to make his pitch fast, Bradley started to speak, but Chester interrupted. "Hello, Good-bye. Bradley is a shit-head."

Bradley looked both surprised and offended. "Nice things you're teaching the bird to say."

"I didn't teach him that. He just picked it up."

"Oh? I suppose people all over town are saying it."

"No," replied Janie. "Just people on the Upper East Side, and parts of Westchester and Long Island."

She had made her point. Bradley let it drop.

"What's he doing back here, anyway?" he grumbled.

"*He* lives here."

Bradley sighed. Things weren't going at all the way he had envisioned. Somehow he had managed to convince himself on the way over that she would have had time to calm down in the last few days, even that she might be just a little pleased to see him. He had been wrong, of course. "Look, I just came here to talk—"

"And I just went to the synagogue to get married." Her tone was light but it carried the full weight of her feelings just the same.

Bradley began to turn red. "I—I'm sorry about that. That's why I came over here tonight. I wanted to apologize. About the baby and—"

"Apologize?" replied Janie, savoring the word as though it had some strange and alien flavor. "You can *apologize* for stepping on my foot. You can *apologize* for your father being late. You can even *apologize* for being unfaithful to me all those months. But a baby . . . a baby you can't *apologize* for." She turned and went down the hall into the kitchen.

Chester rolled his wicked orange eyes in Bradley's direction, gave his best diabolical parrot chuckle and took off after her.

Bradley stood still. He felt like a stranger in his own land. A very unwelcome stranger. Then he heard her running the tap. He heard the sound of dishes clattering against one another in the sink. He took a deep breath and marched forward.

She had her back to the door, both hands in the soapy sink.

"I was not unfaithful to you," he stated, standing in the kitchen doorway.

She stopped washing the cups but left her hands in the water. She did not turn around. "Oh? You and another woman had a child together. What would you call it? A pledge of your love for me?"

Bradley sighed. "It's not like I ever . . . I mean I never even . . . It was only a plastic cup as far as I was concerned."

Janie shook the suds off her hands and turned to face him. "What you *put* it in is not really the issue here, is it?"

"What do you mean? It's not as though I *enjoyed* myself. It's not as though I did it for pleasure."

"Whether or not you enjoyed yourself isn't the point either," cried Janie.

"Well what is the goddamn point, then?" demanded Bradley, who was getting upset because he couldn't defend his position if he didn't know what it was.

"The point is, that (a) you deliberately kept what you were doing a secret from me all that time—"

"I wanted to surprise you."

"Believe me, I was surprised. My mother and father were surprised.

My whole family is positively reeling from the surprise." She reached for a dish towel to dry her hands. "And (b) whether you put it in a plastic cup or a banana daiquiri, and whether you enjoyed yourself or not, *you* have a baby. And I'm not about to raise another woman's child. If I want to devote that much time and energy to a child, I'll have one of my own. Now, if there's nothing else . . ." She waved a hand in the direction of the front door.

Bradley held his ground. "Don't you love me anymore?"

Janie sighed. He would have to bring up emotion and spoil her logical argument. "Whether I love you is not the issue here. As it happens, I probably still do, more or less. But I've thought it over and I realize that I can't live with you and whatsitsname. I'm being honest and I want you to know that, my anger aside, I think it would be false of me to try and pretend I can accept this situation when I can't. I'm sorry, but that is how I feel.

"Janie, I—" He took a step forward.

"No." She held up her hands to shield herself. "Now please leave, before I do something dumb and decide to let you stay." They were brave words, but her voice was breaking.

He looked at her standing there in the kitchen, her face flushed, her eyes brimming with unshed tears, and he knew he had probably never loved her more than he did right then. It was the first time in all the years he had known her that she had displayed any sort of vulnerability at all. The first time that she was not Janie the corporate woman, but just Janie the woman who had suddenly found that there are some things in life you can't control, that sometimes, no matter how careful you are, the balance sheet just doesn't come out right. "I'm sorry," he said, and he meant sorry for both of them. And he turned and went to the front door.

"Bradley is a shithead," crowed Chester triumphantly.

"No, he is not!" cried Janie, throwing another peanut at the parrot and listening as the front door opened and closed.

Two hours later, unable to sleep from too much coffee and too many emotions, Janie got out of bed, got dressed and went for a walk.

It was a cold, still night, clear enough to see the tiny pinpoints of distant stars even from the bottom of Manhattan's blazing pit. She walked north for no particular reason, and after a few blocks she found that she was feeling a little better. Colder, but better. Still, at least walking was *doing* something and anything was better than sitting at home listening to the silence of her life folding itself around her like some large, contented cat. At least out here there was some sound, some life, even at this hour. Suddenly, amid the comforting bleats of the taxis and the hissing of the warm geysers of subcity steam as they erupted from the manholes, she heard another sound. A dog barking.

She stopped and looked around. It was late for anyone to be out walking a dog. And then ahead, in the next block and walking toward her, she saw a dark stocky figure preceded by a bouncing white ball of fluff. They both looked familiar even from this distance, and she smiled slightly and began to walk toward them. Evidently she was not the only one who preferred to ward off the chill within with the cold without.

"Hello, Steve," she said, drawing abreast of the figure.

Steve Curtis's thoughts were miles away, in Fairfield, Connecticut, to be exact. He was preoccupied with examining the most recent blow to his parental status. His ex-wife, Brenda, had called earlier in the evening to say that Bethany and Jared had decided that they wanted to call their stepfather, Bubba, "Daddy" from now on, and she just wanted him to know. Steve had spent the rest of the night trying to find the term for how he felt about that piece of news. By one o'clock he had found it. *Lousy*. And that was why he was out walking Tony in the middle of this cold, cold night. That was also why he didn't even hear his own name the first time Janie called him.

She tried again. "Steve?"

He looked up from beneath the brim of his hat, but before he could even recognize the source of the voice Tony was dancing up and down on his hind legs in greeting. Janie reached down and patted him on the head and, satisfied, he snuggled up next to Janie's booted foot, under the hem of her fur coat.

"Janie?" asked Steve, not believing his own eyes.

"It's me," she said, giving a crooked little smile. She was glad to see him in one way and sad in another. Only pain brought people out walking at this time of night, and Steve Curtis was a nice man. She didn't like to think of him suffering any more than he already had, but those big puppy-dog eyes told her that he was. "What're you doing out on a night like this?

Steve indicated the bichon. "Walking the dog."

"At two a.m.?"

Steve grinned. "You're right. It's more like the other way around. I couldn't sleep and he's keeping me company."

"Where's Lavinia?" It was too cold to stand still, and so they automatically began to walk.

"She's on another buying trip to Europe," replied Steve, though he didn't sound too interested. "But even if she wasn't, she's not the type who wants to know you in the middle of the night. Says she needs her beauty rest or whatever."

"Oh," said Janie. "And what about Marilyn?"

"Lavinia didn't want her and Tony fooling around and making little bichons while she was gone, so she sent Marilyn to stay with a friend who has a spayed bitch. God forbid we should have a litter of pups, eh, Tony? I mean, it might interfere with her plans."

Janie thought he sounded bitter. Evidently nothing had been resolved on the home front.

"Where's your husband?" asked Steve a few moments later. "I should have thought a new bride would have something better to do at this time of the night."

Janie stopped walking. "I don't have a husband."

Steve stopped walking too. "What happened?"

Janie shook her head. "It's a long story."

"I've got all night. Look," he continued, "my place is right around the corner on the next block. Why don't I make us a couple of cups of hot chocolate and you can tell me about it."

"No, I don't think I'd better . . ." said Janie, automatically waving the suggestion aside.

"I'm an excellent listener," coaxed Steve.

Tony sat looking up at the two of them.

But Janie was still not sure. "No, really, I . . ."

Tony got to his feet and, pulling sharply on the leash, slipped it out of Steve's grasp and took off in the direction of his home.

Steve looked at Jane. "I think we'd better go with him, he doesn't have a key." And so the two of them chased Tony all the way home.

CHAPTER TEN

MAXINE SMOOTHED A NONEXISTENT WRINKLE out of her skirt, examined her nails and decided that, babies and nail polish being mutually exclusive alternatives, there was no point in even considering the possibility of a manicure for some time to come. With a sigh she curled the fingers of her right hand under the palm so she wouldn't have to look at the ragged cuticles and then switched the telephone from her left ear to her right because Doris was literally talking her left ear off.

"But, Doris . . . Doris . . ." She kept trying to get a word in. But Doris wasn't ready to surrender control of the conversation just yet. Maxine sighed again and looked at her watch. It was eleven-fifteen. Doris had been deluging her with pleas for intervention, requests for advice and other motherly meanderings for half an hour.

"Doris, I . . . Doris, look I . . ." Then Doris paused to replenish her oxygen supply, and Maxine plunged head-first into the welcome silence. "I told you I'll do what I can. But I think you should know that Bradley seems to think that Janie is seeing someone else."

Doris gasped. "Another man?" she squeaked incredulously.

Maxine nodded. "Hmm-hmm. Of course, he's blinded by jealousy, so I'm not sure whether he actually saw what he thinks he saw, but he's been hanging around outside her house and he said he saw her out walking with a man and his dog. And later he saw the man going into the house with her. What's that? No, I don't know who it is. Bradley seems to think he's seen the man somewhere, but he's not sure where." Doris said something then. "Look, why don't you just ask her who it is?" replied Maxine. "What do you mean, you're afraid she'll tell you it's none of your business? Of course it's *your* business, you're her mother."

But Doris was not convinced.

"I know I'm Dear Maxine," replied Maxine to Doris's next suggestion, "but you're not asking for advice, you're asking for information. You need a detective, not a columnist."

Maxine was trying to inject a little humor into the conversation, but Doris was the product of generations of women whose primary emotional response was not laughter but tears. She took offense.

"Of course I'm not making fun," placated Maxine. "Yes, I know how concerned you are . . . Doris, I *know* what it's like to be a mother, believe me."

Unplacated, Doris went off on another tirade, and with a sigh Maxine rested the receiver against her shoulder, sure that she would not be needed to comment for several minutes.

She looked at the pile of unread letters on her desk. Ever since the wedding she had had trouble concentrating on her work. Somehow other people's problems seemed so much less immediate than her own. And the fact that she couldn't seem to solve the crisis that was pervading her own life made any attempts to do the same for other people seem equally futile. And that included Doris.

Why, she wondered as she stared out the window that formed one wall of her office, had she ever thought that beyond divorce lay freedom, freedom from responsibility for other people, freedom to live for herself instead of for others? She had more people depending on her now than she had when she was married. She began to tick off the names. Bradley, Bradley's baby, Harry, Doris . . .

In the window of the office in the building across the way, a woman was working diligently at her desk, head bent in blissful concentration. Maxine wondered briefly if she had any children. And then decided that if she did, they probably were celibate and lived in another country.

She turned her head away, listened briefly at the earpiece and heard Doris start in on a diatribe on the perils of casual sex. A flash of something in the corner of her eye caught her attention. She swiveled her chair to face the doorway. The pale, puffy face of her wife-in-law smiled wanly at her. Maxine added Joyce's name to her list.

"Can I come in?" asked Joyce, easing herself past the open top drawer of the filing cabinet and sinking into the chair.

Maxine was not really surprised to see her. Joyce's condition, as they used to call it, seemed somehow inexorably bound to her own at the moment. Both of them were having their lives turned upside down by their children, born, unborn, or newly born. And both of them had married Harry. She wondered if there was any connection there. And decided that after all it was motherhood and not the man that was the real link.

She held up the telephone receiver and let it dangle a few inches above the desk. The far-away babble of the loquacious Doris sounded like the chattering of distant gerbils. Maxine mouthed the words "Janie's mother," and Joyce nodded understandingly.

Poor Maxine, thought Joyce. The aftermath of the wedding was still sending ripples through the pool of her life. It had even got to the point where she was bringing Bradley's offspring to work with her in spite of a company policy to the contrary. Of course, Harry could hardly complain under the circumstances, and in fact his only comment to Joyce on the new addition to Maxine's office had been that this ex-wife thought that daycare was no place to leave a baby. And when he had suggested that maybe Bradley could take care of the baby during the day, Maxine had fixed him with one of her looks. The one that suggested that the arteries in his brain were hardening even as they spoke. Harry had wisely decided to let the subject drop.

Joyce mouthed back a question. "Where's the baby?"

Maxine hooked a thumb in the direction of the filing cabinet, and with some effort Joyce got to her feet. She peered into the open top drawer, and sure enough there was Rogue Kraft filed under B for baby and sleeping the peaceful sleep of the totally unconcerned.

She threw a questioning look at Maxine.

"Where else?" Maxine whispered, waving an arm around the cramped space that was her office.

Suddenly both women realized that the gerbil chorus emanating from the telephone receiver had stopped. Maxine cradled the phone under her ear again. "Doris?" She queried into the silence. "Yes, of course I was listening. But I have to go now. Someone's just come into my office." And before Doris had a chance to protest Maxine hung up.

"That woman is driving me insane!" she cried.

Joyce nodded her understanding. "At least you're not related to her now," she offered as a consolation.

"Thank God for small mercies. What more does she think I can do about it? I'm already looking after the baby." She gestured toward the filing cabinet. "Not to mention its father. Now she wants me to go over there and talk to her daughter, do my Dear Maxine shtick and make it all work out all right. Honestly! What does she think I'm going to do? Wave a magic wand and make *that* disappear?" She pointed at the open drawer.

Still nodding her understanding in some kind of rote response, Joyce felt a sudden wave of nausea grip her, and she instinctively put a hand over the cause of it. What little color there had been in her face drained away.

"You feel sick?" asked Maxine, although she already knew the answer. "What about the soda crackers I told you to eat?"

Joyce took a deep breath before attempting to answer her. "I . . . I tried that but . . ." She swallowed back another wave of sickness. "I thought this was supposed to be *morning sickness.* This lasts all day and all night too. My stomach feels like I'm living on a roller coaster!"

"Some women have it worse than others," agreed Maxine matter-of-factly. "It should pass by the time you get to the fourth month, though."

Joyce shook her head.

"No, I mean it," replied Maxine, misinterpreting the negative response. "By the fourth month you should start feeling much better, more energy, less tired, not so sick. You'll see." She smiled the big bright smile of the cheerfully nonpregnant.

A glimmer of hope crossed Joyce's face.

But in the interest of accuracy Maxine continued. "Of course, that's when your hair will probably start falling out."

Joyce looked appropriately stricken. Her hair had always been her best feature. "My *hair* will start falling out?"

Maxine realized she had said the wrong thing. "Sometimes, not always. With some women it's the hair. With others it's stretch marks or varicose veins." She shrugged, apologizing for being the bearer of bad tidings, but getting in deeper every minute in spite of herself.

"Stretch marks! Varicose veins!" croaked Joyce.

Maxine nodded. "But it doesn't happen to everyone. With me it was hemorrhoids."

"Hemorrhoids!" Joyce sounded stricken. She wasn't ready to join the Preparation H brigade just yet. "I never knew—I mean, I thought women were supposed to glow when they were pregnant. You know, Mother Nature, natural biological functions, all that stuff." She knew nothing about pregnancy, had never wanted to know anything about it. And in fact the entire thrust of her education and experience in the area of conception had been focused on how to avoid it. What happened if you failed to achieve this avoidance had never really been discussed.

When she went to high school, sex education had consisted solely of admonitions not to. Of course, everyone had known what happened to girls who did, but they never talked about it in any detail. The guilty girl simply went away to stay with an aunt in another state and several months later she came back—alone. The only obvious side effect of the pregnancy had been that these girls got excused from Phys. Ed. whenever they wanted to without having to bring a note from home. Nobody ever said anything about going bald.

And later there had been the pill. This had precluded the need to know anything about being pregnant as long as one could count to twenty-one. And as for pregnant friends, anybody Joyce had ever known who had chosen to procreate had done so quietly and unobtrusively, in the suburbs where the side effects had been buffered by the distance. Added to that was the fact that Joyce had never planned on having a pregnancy of her own and therefore felt no need to become better informed. The same as she had never bothered to learn about the idiosyncrasies of foreign cars because she never planned to own one. Now, therefore, at the age of forty-two she found herself both ignorant and pregnant.

Maxine sniffed with derision. "I never knew a woman yet who glowed. Bad breath, yes. Loose teeth, sure. But glowing, uh-uh."

"No glowing?" said Joyce, sounding disappointed and relieved at the same time. For the past several days she had been worried that what was happening to her was abnormal. "Besides not glowing, is there anything else I should know?"

"Are you sure you're ready for it?" inquired Maxine ominously.

Joyce nodded, but with very little enthusiasm.

The older woman plunged on. "Well, you should know that some women get pregnancy amnesia. You know, they can't remember telephone numbers, dates, where they put things."

"You mean I'm going to lose my mind as well as my hair!" cried Joyce, trying to envision how she was going to continue to write without the former or go out in public without the latter.

"Not your mind. Just your memory," corrected Maxine.

But Joyce didn't hear her. She was busy trying to remember where she had put the notes from her last interview.

Maxine continued. "And then also you should stay out of the sun. Pregnancy mask takes a long time to fade, if it fades at all. And your feet will probably get bigger, so you shouldn't plan on being whatever size you were before, after."

"Pregnancy mask?" Joyce seemed to be getting smaller in her chair with each new piece of information. "Bigger feet?" Until now the only physical side effect of pregnancy that she had been aware of was fatness. What Maxine was talking about sounded more like some sort of demented decrepitude. "There isn't anything else, is there?" she pleaded.

"Any or all of the above and that's about it. Oh, and there's heartburn, of course."

"Of course."

"But those are the only ones I can remember. It's been a long time since I was pregnant."

"That's enough, believe me." Joyce swallowed hard again, forcing down the bile that was rising in her throat. "Why would anyone want to go through something like that on purpose?"

Maxine gave a little grin. "As I remember it, most of us didn't have a choice. It just happened. And while we're on the subject—" She raised her eyebrows in a question.

A little color began to return to Joyce's face. "It was the night before I went to China. It was late. It was cold. I couldn't face getting out of bed and running into the bathroom. And I hate using the diaphragm anyway. It's so slippery. Half the time it goes flying across the room like some sort of prophylactic Frisbee."

They both smiled at the image, sharing for a moment the conspiratorial in-joke that all women understand as the true meaning of sex.

"I thought, well you know, just this one time won't hurt." Joyce finished with a shrug.

Maxine smiled. "Welcome to the club, honey."

Joyce was serious again. "What's it like being a mother?"

"Well, let's just put it this way. After pregnancy comes childbirth. The terrible twos. Adolescence."

Joyce held up her hands to silence her. "Enough, enough, no more information. I don't think I can handle it right now."

Maxine acquiesced. She was beginning to depress herself. She had thought about adding adulthood to the list because of her own situation with Bradley. Then she decided that he was probably still covered under adolescence.

"It's a big commitment, isn't it?" said Joyce in a very small voice.

Maxine picked up something in the tone that set her on guard. "Joyce, why did you really come to see me today?"

For a moment Joyce said nothing. The silence in the room was broken only by the hiss of heated air from the vents below the window.

"Joyce?"

Joyce took a deep breath. "I—" she cleared her throat. "That is . . ."

"Are you thinking about *not* having this baby?" asked Maxine quietly.

"How did you guess?" Joyce seemed surprised.

"I'm Dear Maxine, remember?" said Maxine with just a hint of irony.

"Well, as a matter of fact, I had thought about getting—"

"Was it something I said?"

Joyce shook her head.

Maxine continued to explain. "The side effects, they're not *that* bad. Really."

Joyce gave a little smile. "No, it's not that. It's me. I don't know anything about being a mother. I like my career. I like my life the way it is. So I thought . . ."

"What does Harry say?"

"Not much."

"Not much!"

Joyce fidgeted in her chair. "I mean, I haven't had a chance to really sit down and talk to him about it. And anyway, he's acting funny lately. Every time I say I feel sick, he says he feels sick. I'm exhausted, but he sleeps more than I do. And you know what else?"

"He has cravings."

"How did you know?" asked Joyce in surprise.

"Harry and I were pregnant once too."

"What do you mean, you *and* Harry?"

"Some men get more involved in their wives' pregnancies than others. And I'm not just talking about Lamaze classes here. They call it the Couvade Syndrome. It means that some husbands of pregnant women mirror the symptoms of the pregnancy."

"You're kidding," cried Joyce in disbelief. And then she laughed. "Harry can't afford to lose any hair."

Maxine grinned back at her. "Listen, with me he even had labor pains. We thought it was an ulcer until the doctor explained it. Harry is a real family man." And as she said it she suddenly recalled the night when he had offered to help her bathe Bradley's baby. Maybe having a baby with Joyce was just what he needed to get over his continuing attachment to her. And then, like a computer working out a problem, her brain spat out another premise for examination. Maybe it wasn't her he was attached to but the family they had been. Maybe that's what kept Harry mooning over their marriage. It was a possibility worth considering. And so she chose her next words carefully.

"Joyce, I think you should sit down and have a serious talk with

Harry about what you're feeling. It wouldn't be fair to either of you for you to make this decision on your own."

Joyce sighed. "You're right. But then I knew that's what you'd say." She thought for a moment. "Do you think Harry wants this baby?"

"You won't know for sure unless you ask him. But my guess would be that he does. Or at least he will when he gets over the shock of becoming a grandfather and a father in the same year." Maxine looked at her watch. "Oh my God!"

"What?"

"It's after twelve. I've got to be at the Ladies Press Club luncheon in ten minutes. I'm the speaker." Quickly Maxine grabbed her purse and stood up. She was looking directly into the baby drawer. "The baby!" She turned to Joyce. "Would you mind? Just until I get back. I'll only be an hour or so." And Maxine grabbed her jacket from the hook behind the door.

"But I—" Joyce started to protest, but Maxine was already on her way out the door. "What do I *do* with it?" cried Joyce after her.

Maxine paused in the hallway. "If it's wet, change it. If it's hungry feed it, and if it cries, pick it up." And with that she was gone.

Stunned by the sudden responsibility, Joyce sat for a moment to gather her thoughts. She was an only child. As a teenager she had never babysat for anything but plants, houses and pets. In short, while she may have traveled to the far corners of the earth and been alone with all manner of famous and infamous people in the course of doing her interviews, she had never been alone with a *baby* before.

"It it's wet, change it. If it's hungry, feed it. If it cries, pick it up," she repeated Maxine's instructions like a comforting litany once or twice more and then she stood up and looked into the drawer.

Rogue Kraft was awake now, and he looked back at her with great blue-eyed solemnity as if summing up her abilities as a substitute caretaker. And Joyce had the definite impression that he knew perfectly well she had never been alone with a baby before. She could see it in his eyes.

"Hello, baby," she cooed softly. "It's me, Joyce, remember? But Maxine will be right back so please, please, don't need anything until she gets here, O.K.?"

Rogue Kraft appeared to sum up this appeal for a few seconds. Then his face creased and began to turn red. He waved his plump pink fists frantically in the air, grunted and then opened his toothless cave of a mouth and released a piercing wail of discomfort. Even Joyce recognized it as such, though she had no idea what was happening until, a few seconds later, a decidedly unpleasant odor began to suffuse first the filing drawer and then the rest of the office. It made her already tender stomach lurch with protest. Briefly she leaned against the filing cabinet for support. And then she did the only thing she could do. She reached into the drawer, extracted the baby and looked around for a fresh supply of diapers, which as it happened were in the next drawer down, filed under D.

CHAPTER ELEVEN

MAXINE WAS WEARING HER "GOOD" BLACK DRESS—the one with the sophisticated padded shoulders and the moderately plunging V—which made her short neck seem longer and, let's face it, more youthful; the pearls Harry had given her for their tenth anniversary and which only saw the light of day on special occasions; a pair of textured panty hose patterned with those little fuzzy dots that looked as though some sort of alien lifeform was flourishing on them; and heels that were a good inch higher than the ones she normally wore. She looked in the mirror to study the effect. It had been a long time since she had gotten ready for a date, but even so, instinct told her that something wasn't quite right.

"I look like I'm going to an Italian funeral," she muttered irritably and then did a half turn so she could examine her reflection from another angle. Maybe she looked better from the rear. Not that that would do any good unless she wanted to spend the evening walking backward. But the new angle didn't make her look any better.

"It just doesn't look like *me*," she complained and tugged at the shoulder pads, pulling them up. That made a difference. Not that she looked more like her. But at least she looked like somebody. She looked like Marcus Allen. She pushed the shoulder pads sideways a little. Hello, "Maxine Dearest." She slumped with a sigh. The pads settled back toward her spine. Bending slightly from the waist and raising one limp-wristed arm, she did a reasonable impression of Charles Laughton. "The bells, the bells!" she cackled and then broke into a little grin. Getting ready for a date with a younger man required a sense of humor, no doubt about it. Then she tore the shoulder pads, which were fortunately only attached by Velcro, from their moorings and threw them on the bed. There, that was better. Or was it?

She took another long, appraising look at the woman in the mirror and then unhooked the pearls. There was something about pearls that always said "Aunt Margaret." And whatever she might or might not want to say to Jeffrey Mondavi, it was not that.

Fishing around in her jewelry box, she came up with a pair of dangling faux-diamond earrings that she had bought on a sortie to Ciros one Saturday afternoon after having one of those *consoling* single lunches with two of her divorced friends. She put these on, decided that the effect was definitely more up to date, and then sat down and took off the fuzzy dotted stockings. These she replaced with a plain pair that advertised itself as Night Nude, Size B. Standing once more, she studied herself in the mirror again.

"Now I look like I'm going to an Italian wedding!" She was still not satisfied with the way she looked, although common sense told her that if she took off anything else she would be down to her underwear, and you couldn't go to dinner in your underwear, not even in New York City.

But more important than how she looked was why she cared so much about how she looked. After all, this date had originally been to get Harry off her back. But new developments on the Joyce front seemed to be taking care of that quite nicely. In fact, she hadn't even heard from her ex-husband in several days. This she took as a good sign. So why was she still going out with Jeffrey Mondavi? Why was she going out and leaving her *son* in charge of his son—for the first time? Why was she so concerned about the way she looked? And why was she having so much trouble getting it right?

And then it hit her: because she had no idea what Maxine—the woman—was *supposed* to look like. Oh, she knew what Harry's wife was supposed to look like. And she knew what Bradley's mother and even Rogue's grandmother was supposed to look like, because she saw that woman in the mirror every day. She even had a pretty good idea of what Dear Maxine was supposed to look like (and here she included the pearls), but none of these women was going out with Jeffrey Mondavi, a man from another generation. And the last time Maxine had had to dress *Maxine* for a date with a man had been twenty-eight years ago. But she knew that what worked then would not work now. Besides, she had no idea what had happened to the felt circle skirt with the poodle appliqué. And she had even less of an idea why, her other motives having receded, she was still going out with him.

Bradley stuck his head around her bedroom door. "Hey, Ma, you look fantastic!"

"You think so?" Maxine tugged at the neck of the dress, pulling up the bodice so that the V wasn't quite so low. She wondered if maybe a scarf would look all right. It *was* cold outside. And it would stop Jeffrey from letting his eyes wander down the front of her dress if he were so inclined.

She turned to her son. "You think maybe a scarf?"

Bradley shook his head. "Scarves are for old ladies. You look great just the way you are."

"You're sure the earrings aren't too much?" She shook her head and little lasers of light bounced around the room.

"The earrings are perfect." He came and stood behind her. "Ma, are you nervous about going out with him?"

"Nervous? Why should I be nervous? Just because the last time I had dinner with a man other than your father it was like *The Night of the Living Dead.* Just because I'm old enough to be his mother. Just because I'm leaving you alone with the baby." She turned to face him. "Are you sure you don't want me to get a babysitter? Someone who knows what to do?"

"I can handle a sleeping baby, Ma. You've already bathed him and changed him and fed him. What else can he need?"

Maxine wasn't convinced. "Maybe I should stay home." She pulled off one earring and then the other.

Bradley took the earrings from her and clipped them back on. "You're going out. You're going to have a good time. You are not going to worry. Besides, one of us has to have a love life and it doesn't look like it's going to be me." As he spoke, he was guiding her out of the bedroom and down the hallway to the front door.

"I'm not having a love life. I'm just having dinner." The thought that her son thought that she would actually consider going to bed with anyone other than his father was a disturbing one. Even in light of current circumstances, she still felt that her son shouldn't *know* his parents did those kinds of things with each other, never mind other people. The idea that Bradley had ever envisioned the act that created him had embarrassed Maxine ever since she knew he was old enough to. For that reason she had never been able to bring herself to have that talk with him about where babies come from. And as she later found out, neither had Harry. Which, considering how her grandson arrived, had evidently been a mistake. Maybe it wasn't too late . . .

While she was pondering that possibility, Bradley was getting her coat from the hall closet, helping her into it and steering her as far as the front door. "Have a good time, Ma. You deserve it."

She looked into his face. His remark surprised her. Since when had he shown any interest in her personal enjoyment of anything? He was her child and as such he had always been preoccupied with his own selfish self-interest. She had accepted that. As a mother she felt it was her job, part of the natural order of things. But now what did she see in those eyes that hovered a few inches above her own? Was that a flicker of maturity, the faint and distant glint of an emerging adult? Or was it just that the light bulb in the vestibule needed changing? "Bradley, I . . ."

He put both his hands on her tiny shoulders and looked down into her face. "Ma, I haven't said anything before. I guess because I've been too wrapped up in my own problems. But I really do appreciate what you've done for me . . . and for Rogue. I know it's been a lot of work and I know I haven't been much help. I promise I'll try and do more.

Reaching up, she stroked her palm along the side of his face and finished it off with a little motherly pat. "You're a good boy, Bradley. A good boy."

He opened the door to let her out. "Knock him dead, Ma," he said, and he watched her walk down the hall to the elevators, tottering just a little on the unfamiliar heels.

The China Grill is located on West 53rd Street on the ground floor of the CBS Building. Because of this prestigious connection to a major network, the place attracts those who wish to eat as well as those who wish to be seen while they are eating and those who wish to observe those who wish to be seen. It was, in other words, just the sort of place where Jeffrey Mondavi loved to hang out.

When Maxine arrived, therefore, Jeffrey was already hanging out, leaning casually against the long bar, looking every inch the successful young Manhattan male. He was dressed in the capacious unicolored uniform of the moment, which is to say that his shirt was the same color as his suit and his tie, and his trousers looked like there was enough room inside for at least one more person.

Maxine saw him before he saw her because he was busy being *seen* by a table occupied by four young women who seemed to consist mostly of long hair and longer legs. She hesitated by the door for a moment, undecided whether to plow on through the crowd or stand there and wait until his eyes wandered in her direction. While she was waiting to be discovered, she looked around. She had never been to the China Grill before, or for that matter to any place that even vaguely resembled it.

From the towering ceiling hung a series of elliptical objects that may have been either light fixtures or a fleet of hovering extraterrestrial vehicles. An underwater effect was created by the stillwater-green of the soaring marbleized walls and the sunken-city-of-Atlantis tessellated floor, through which wandered a series of quotations from the journals of Marco Polo, in long, thin snakes of darker tile. Maxine didn't know that was what they were, of course, and probably wouldn't have cared if she had—the only Polo that she was on familiar terms with was the brand name.

She wondered briefly if she might be any good at writing restaurant reviews. But after a few moments of silently reciting her impressions of the decor, she realized that this might become a permanent pastime if she waited for Jeffrey to come and get her, or even to notice that she had arrived. So, with more bravado than she actually felt, she pushed her way through the densely packed restaurant, noticing as she went that nearly every woman in the room was wearing black.

At least I got the color right, she thought, approaching on Jeffrey's blind side. And it wasn't until she placed a tentative hand on his arm that he became aware of her at all.

"Jeffrey?" It was half question, half greeting.

"Maxine!" He turned at the sound of his name and then swooped down and gave her a big kiss on the cheek, nearly knocking her off balance. Then he moved back a little and looked at her. "I always said you were the best-looking woman at *Destiny*. And trust you to know that Bleak Chic is all the rage in this place. Black is back with a vengeance this season."

The compliment relaxed her a little, as did the fact that he had now completely turned his back on the table of four girls. He looped a proprietary arm around her waist. "Love the earrings, *chérie*," he whispered, leaning close and letting his hot breath fog up the faux for a few seconds. "Care for a drink?"

Maxine decided that a drink was definitely what she cared for—probably two—compliments and attention being relaxing only to a certain point. She did a half turn to look behind the bar, feeling as she did so the warm form of Jeffrey Mondavi closing in behind her with the silent precision of a bank vault thumping shut. But she dismissed the increased proximity, putting it down to the fact that the China Grill was not much less crowded than the country from which it drew its name.

She occupied her attention instead with the activity behind the bar. At one end was an open kitchen with perhaps a dozen chefs and chefettes frantically stir-frying, grilling and wokking and then tossing their results with vast quantities of rice or noodles. To Maxine it looked as though they were not so much *cooking* the food as *assembling* it, which was to her indicative not just of the current state of the kitchen but of the society in which it existed. Nobody had time to do things the old-fashioned way anymore. A trend that seemed to apply equally to eating and procreating.

At the other end of the bar, where she was standing with the increasingly proximate Jeffrey, an impressive array of bottles testified to the international tastes of the clientele. And on the back wall were additional glass shelves to accommodate the dozens of exotic liqueurs and liquors that were no doubt de rigueur with the Bleak Chic set, including one whole shelf given over to imported single malt scotches with names like Cardhu, Glenfargh, Knockando and Laphroaig, the pronunciations of which were difficult at best and no doubt impossible if consumed. Maxine imagined that even an aficionado would be reduced to ordering "another third from the left for me and a second from the right for my friend" after not too many drinks.

She turned to Jeffrey. "What are you drinking?" she asked, eyeing the half-empty square glass that sat before him on the bar.

"Water."

"Water?"

"Well, actually, it's Rokko," he said, rounding the *o* and letting both *k*'s catch briefly in the back of his throat.

Maxine looked puzzled.

"Japanese mineral water," he explained and then added, "It's the most expensive one they have. Six bucks a bottle."

"Six dollars for a little bottle of water!" Maxine had some trouble swallowing that. She thought to herself, when I was first married, for six dollars I could feed Harry and me for a week. She said to Jeffrey, "If they charge six dollars for water, what do they charge for the drinks?"

"What difference does it make? My women go first-class—all the way." And he gave her a little wink. "You like wine? They have a very good California Chardonnay here, Grgich Hills, Napa Valley '84. Or if you like French, the Chassagne Montrachet '85 is excellent."

His accent was perfect and perfectly rehearsed. Maxine had the definite impression that he had said the same line a few times before. Probably in front of the bathroom mirror.

"Are you going to have some?" Since her own experience with wine did not extend much beyond Mogen David, Maxine was uncertain which if either she should choose so that her vineal ignorance would not be quite so obvious.

Jeffrey shook his head. "I never touch alcohol," he stated monastically and then added, looking deep into her eyes, his pupils contracting to tiny thrusting dark points, "I find it dulls the senses." And he let the word *senses* linger on his tongue, ending it with a slight sibilance as he pushed the tip of his tongue suggestively against the gap in his front teeth.

"I'll have a vodka and tonic," said Maxine, quickly looking away. "With lime."

By the time their table was ready Maxine had had two vodka and tonics, and Jeffrey had done his bit for the trade deficit, matching her drink for drink with his imported designer water. She was feeling better and he was feeling her, with little rubs and pats here and there. Rather, she reflected, basking in the warm glow of the vodka, in the same way one pinches a melon to see if it is not overripe.

For the most part, though, she ignored these little liberties because Jeffrey, as it turned out, was an excellent listener, and it had been a long time since she had had anybody who wanted to listen to *her*. So if he did lean in a little closer than necessary to do it, well, having an attractive young man draped over you wasn't the worst way to pass an evening. It was certainly better than having someone named Rogue spit up on your neck.

But watching all that food being *assembled* behind the bar, smelling the exotic smells of ginger and cilantro, soy and curry, had set her taste buds reeling off onto tangents of anticipated pleasure. At the moment, food and not conversation was her ultimate desire. When the waiter brought the menus, she was more than ready to order.

Jeffrey perused his menu like the expert that he was. Although he already knew what he was going to order, he liked the effect of looking like he was making up his mind anew. Then he waited politely for Maxine to give hers the once-over. It didn't take long before she put her menu back on the table.

"Do you know what you want?" he asked, rubbing warm fingers over the top of her hand. And Maxine had the fleeting impression that he was talking about more than just food. But her appetite ruled the moment, and she ignored the implications in his touch and relayed her order. Jeffrey in turn beckoned to the waiter who had been hovering discreetly nearby.

"The lady will have the sautéed foie gras and the grilled Colorado lamb with the jade sauce. And I'll have the raw Beijing oysters in black sauce and the dry aged Szechuan beef." He handed the menus back to the waiter, who tucked them under his arm and finished writing the order. But before he could leave the table Jeffrey stopped him. "On second thought, make that a *double* order of the oysters." Both he and the waiter looked briefly at Maxine. "And another round of drinks too."

While Jeffrey was busy devouring his second plate of raw oysters, Bradley was frantically searching for the thermometer. Rogue had woken up screaming and hot, and even Bradley, who knew next to nothing about babies, knew a sick one when he saw one. Finally he found it and thrust it into the mouth of his son.

But, as he quickly discovered, taking a baby's temperature is not a simple task. When babies are sick they cry, and when they cry they open their mouths—a lot. And Bradley could not get an accurate reading. Either Rogue had a fever of 104 or a temperature of 82, which meant he was comatose even though he wasn't. Either way, it was a bad sign.

Frantic now and more than a little frightened both by his own ignorance and by the screams emanating from the infant, Bradley did the only thing he could think of. He bundled up the baby and headed for the nearest Emergency Room.

When he got to the hospital, which happened to be called Our Lady of Perpetual Miracles, no doubt a very reassuring name for any who consigned themselves into its care, he was relieved to find that, it not being a full moon, a Saturday night, Halloween or the playoff of a major sports event, instead of the crowd he had expected to find in his what-else-can-go-wrong frame of mind, the Emergency Room was all but empty.

He hurried through the waiting room, across the gray tiled floor, past the drab green walls, the sagging couch and the coffee table with one miserable *Time* magazine folded open at an ad for Blue Cross and rushed up to the desk, which harbored a large black woman encased in a blindingly white uniform, her hair pulled back in a tight, tight bun. The deskplate announced "Admitting Nurse"; her nameplate defined her as Miss McAdams.

"Can I help you?" she rumbled in a voice deeper than anything Bradley had heard since the last time he had seen an interview with Larry Holmes.

"It's my baby. He's sick," cried Bradley, stating the obvious and thrusting the bundle that was Rogue forward for inspection.

Nurse McAdams waved the bundle aside. "Have a seat," she boomed, indicating the lone worn chair in front of her desk with one hand and extracting a fresh yellow form from her drawer with the other, a gesture she performed with all the grace of a symphony conductor leading his favorite orchestra.

Obediently, Bradley sat down, cuddling Rogue protectively to him, overwhelmed with feelings of guilt, fear and something that, had he been a mother, he would have identified immediately as maternal instinct. The baby had stopped crying now, and Bradley found that even more alarming. "I don't know what's wrong. He—he's got a temperature, I think, and—"

"The *doctor* will decide what is wrong with the child," stated Nurse McAdams, evoking the name of the all-powerful being in the slightly musical cadence that evokes visions of palm trees and beaches and still blue seas. "But first we have to fill out this form." She picked up a well-sharpened pencil. "Your name?"

"Kraft, Bradley Kraft. Look, couldn't we see a doctor first?"

"*First*, we will fill out the form." Nurse McAdams peered at him from over the top of her wire-rimmed glasses. It was a look that said that she tolerated no opposition. This was, after all, a hospital, and hospitals are generally not noted for their democratic ideology. She looked back at the form. "Mrs. Kraft's name?"

"Maxine," replied Bradley automatically. And Nurse McAdams wrote down Maxine next to Name of Mother.

"Child's name?"

"Rogue," said Bradley, who was anxious to get this over with and get in to see a doctor, an intern, or even a nurse with a large family.

Nurse McAdams paused and peered over her glasses once more. "Rogue?" She rolled the word off her tongue like it had a bad taste and then smacked her ample lips together as if to clear further traces of it from her mouth.

"Is there a problem with that?" bristled Bradley, who, clutching the hot, hot, baby tighter in his arms, was in no mood for explanations or excuses.

"Not for me," replied the nurse and wrote down Rogue next to Name of Patient.

"How old is the child?" she asked next, this time without looking up from the form.

"Old?"

She looked up and rephrased the question. "When was he born?"

Bradley swallowed hard. Not surprisingly, fear and worry had replaced common sense. He hadn't anticipated this turn of events. "I don't know?" It was a little voice with just a little question mark at the end of it.

"You don't *know* when your baby was born?" Nurse McAdams put down her pencil and folded her huge hands in front of her like a schoolteacher talking to a naughty pupil.

"I—that is—I was—" stuttered Bradley, searching for an acceptable excuse. "I—was away when it happened."

Her wide black face creased into an enormous, unforgiving frown. "Well, when did your wife"—she consulted the form—"Maxine become pregnant?"

"Maxine!" cried Bradley. "She didn't—I mean, she isn't—"

Nurse McAdams had it in her mind that his mother was his wife. The frown became even more unforgiving. Bradley looked down at the tiny screwed-up face in the blanket. For the sake of expediency he decided he might as well let the nurse go on believing that Maxine was his wife. It had to be easier—and quicker—than trying to explain the truth. And anyway, what harm could it do?

"You see, we were separated for a while . . ." Nurse McAdams could fill in the blank spots herself.

"I see," replied the nurse ominously, and in the margin of the page she wrote "Possible marital problems." "And where is your wife, uh, Maxine, tonight?"

"She's out on a date. I mean she's working late!" The baby had begun to fuss again, and Bradley was having trouble keeping his mind on the questions, never mind the answers. "Can we hurry this up?"

"We can only go as fast as the form will permit," she replied with the stoic acceptance of those who are not in a hurry. And in the margin she also wrote, "Mother works." "Now tell me, what are the child's symptoms?"

"Symptoms. Well, he's very warm and he was crying when he woke up and I tried to take his temperature but . . ."

"Did you use a rectal thermometer?"

"A rectal thermometer? No, I mean, I didn't know . . ."

"You should have used a rectal thermometer." She shook her head so forcefully from side to side that Bradley was afraid her hair would snap off.

"Now, Mr. Kraft, we may be dealing with an allergy here. What did you feed the child today?"

"Feed him? Uh . . ." This was a tough one. Maxine always fed the baby something in a bottle. He had no idea exactly what.

"Is your wife breast-feeding?" asked the nurse, trying a different approach.

"Noooo . . ." That was one thing he was sure of.

"Then she is bottle-feeding?" prodded the nurse.

Bradley nodded, glad he could answer one of the questions at last.

"Well, what is *in* the bottle, Mr. Kraft?" asked Nurse McAdams.

"Milk?" offered Bradley hopefully. But the piercing black eyes glaring over the top of the glasses told him that not only had he not answered the $64,000 question but he was in danger of being carted off to the psychiatric ward.

Nurse McAdams shook her tightly tied head again and in the margin at the bottom of the page she wrote, "Possible child neglect or abuse."

CHAPTER TWELVE

JEFFREY MONDAVI let his chocolate-colored eyes drizzle over Maxine's face and down the front of her dress and said, "Are you ready?"

"Ready for what?" In the parlance of her youth this question had usually indicated a desire to take one's date home, but somehow she did not think from the way the evening had been progressing that home-taking was the activity Jeffrey had in mind.

He placed his broad, smooth hand over hers, pressing it lightly but firmly against the cool rigidity of the tabletop. "To go back to your place."

"My place?" Maxine hedged. She needed time to decide an answer. A thousand thoughts ran through her mind, from how tidy was the apartment to what about Bradley. None of these questions was really the issue, of course, but they served as an appropriate diversion and prevented her from having to examine the meat of the moment—to wit, what came after going back to her place? A simple good night at the door? Or was there something more on his mind? And here she was using the word *mind* as a euphemism for an anatomical location considerably south of there.

But seriously, wasn't she just jumping the gun a bit? Maybe all he meant was that he was ready to take her home. End of evening. Good night. See you at the office tomorrow. After all, for her to assume that a man who could have any of the long-haired, long-legged Bleak Chic disciples in the room couldn't wait to go to bed with her, a woman who was old enough to be his mother—but still in pretty good shape—was just a tad presumptuous. Wasn't it?

Her mind fought to find the answer to his question. She was caught between her instincts and her intelligence, her ego and her logic. But all she found was that logic and vodka do not mix, even with lime. In fact, vodka seemed to mix better with instincts, with or without lime. Somewhere inside Maxine the Woman little fires were being fanned. Fires that had been little more than glowing embers for some time. She took a sip from her water glass to douse the flames.

Finally she gave up trying to sort out his motives and decided that since she had no idea what his intentions were she might as well suspend her decision until either her mind or the situation had cleared a bit.

"All right," she agreed, sliding her hand out from under his and reaching for her purse. She realized that, whatever circumstances might arise, she had no need to worry. After all, she had a son and a *grandson* at home waiting for her. It was a situation fraught with safety.

They left the China Grill and walked east along West 53rd Street, past Fifth Avenue, past Madison and onto Lexington before turning north. It was a brisk evening, damp but not too cold, refreshing after the sultry, heavily wokked atmosphere of the restaurant, so rather than hurry, they lingered here and there in front of the window displays.

Most of the stores were getting ready for the four-week shopping frenzy that consumed the citizens of the city between Thanksgiving and Christmas, and so their efforts to attract the passersby were boldly evocative, from origami-covered Christmas trees to dancing elves and scenes from *fin de siècle* New York. It was Maxine's favorite time in Manhattan; a romantic season filled with excitement and hope and— Jeffrey Mondavi's hand?

Jeffrey curled his fingers through her gloved ones. And even through the leather of her glove and the cashmere lining she could feel his heat. Why was it that holding hands was such a different sensation depending on whose hand you were holding? Children's hands. Husband's hands. Friends' hands. Parents' hands. They all felt different. But none of them felt like this. She stole a quick sideways glance at Jeffrey. What *did* he want from her? And more important, what did she want him to want?

At the corner of Lexington and 55th they stopped for a light. And Jeffrey, who was never one to let an opportunity go by, turned to Maxine and gently took hold of her chin, tilted it just a little and placed a soft, searching kiss on her lips.

Well, that answered that question.

He timed the kiss perfectly to coincide with the change in the light. "Green for go," he whispered close to her ear and, still holding her hand, stepped off the curb.

Maxine, still feeling the kiss, still reeling from feelings that she had not felt in a quarter of a century—give or take the first year of her marriage to Harry—trotted along beside him, automatically dodging grates and cracks in the pavement, like the consummate New York pedestrian that she was.

She was sure now that she had not misread the question back in the restaurant and surer still that she had no idea how she was going to handle the situation when she got back home.

Of course there was always Bradley. Having a son was an excellent excuse to avoid asking a man into your apartment. Or at least it used to be. She would simply tell Jeffrey he couldn't come in because Bradley and the baby were there and they would say good night at the door. She had made up her mind. Soft, searching kisses notwithstanding. There was no other way to handle it. The fresh air had cleared her head considerably, and regardless of what Jeffrey had in mind for the climax of their evening, Maxine knew what she was going to do.

But while she was busy mulling over the correct way of saying good night at the door—a practice she had gotten out of the habit of during her marriage—Jeffrey was beginning to feel the effect of the double portion of oysters. He was young. He was single. He was horny as hell. And he couldn't wait to get Maxine out of her coat, out of her dress and into her bed. He stepped up the pace.

Maxine, who was joined to him by her right hand and had no choice but to keep up, began to breathe a little harder as she matched his long strides with her tiny tapping steps. Naturally, Jeffrey took the heavy breathing and her willingness to increase her speed as a sign that she was as anxious to get down to the real business of the evening as he was. And why not? It was common knowledge that divorced women were hot to trot. And he knew that Maxine had been on her own for over a year. A year was a long time to go without a warm body in your bed, even at her age.

After another half a block they reached Maxine's building, and she gratefully paused to catch her breath. "Well, this is where I live," she said brightly, wondering if he was going to kiss her and if the doorman was watching.

"I know," was all Jeffrey said, and he guided her toward the lobby door.

The doorman, who was both conscious and conscientious, was ready and waiting. Christmas was coming. The Season of Giving. The Season of Tipping. He threw open the door with a big, broad smile. "Good evening, Mrs. Kraft. And how are you this foine, foine evening?" he boomed in his best Dublinesque accent.

Maxine had just enough time to nod her response before Jeffrey swept her into the lobby and then into the waiting elevator. She had the distinct feeling that things were beginning to speed up and that somehow she had lost control of events. There was little point in rehearsing how to say good night at the front *door* of the building when you were already in the *elevator*.

As the doors closed on the elevator, Jeffrey pushed the button for her floor.

"How do you know—" she started to ask, but he silenced her with another long, lingering kiss.

"I know," he murmured against her mouth as he let the kiss slip away into an infinity of lip nibbling.

Somewhere in the future, the elevator chimed its destination and Jeffrey took her hand—the other one this time—and led her into the hallway.

"My son is—" she tried to explain, or maybe to protest, but he took her firmly by the shoulders and outside Mrs. Finestein's door he pushed her gently/roughly/insistently against the wall and kissed her again. This time the kiss was longer, harder and she got to meet his tongue and fondle the gap in his front teeth with hers.

Her head was spinning from the last of the vodka, not to mention the physical sensations he was arousing in her as the little flames he had ignited back in the China Grill took hold and became full-fledged fires. This, she reflected ever so briefly as he pressed his body against hers and she allowed logic to have one final say in what was transpiring, must be *passion.*

This was also Mrs. Finestein's wall. And it was beyond the bounds of tenant relations that she should be caught being passionate against Mrs. Finestein's wall. Somewhere, therefore, she found a free hand, and inserting it between the two of them she pried Jeffrey off her.

"Jeffrey—" It had the sound of a strangled protest, partly because his tongue was still doing a tour of her mouth. But he got the message all the same. Or at least he got *a* message—the one that said "Hurry up, let's go to my place *now."* And letting go of her ever so briefly he took her by the arm and hurried her further down the hall.

"Where are your keys?" he demanded with more sexual urgency than she had seen or heard since the Beatles were on the "Ed Sullivan Show."

Caught up in the heat of the moment, she shuffled in her purse. She found her keys. Extracted them. Dropped them. Jeffrey swooped down, picked them up and handed them back to her. In spite of the cold air outside, Maxine could see that his face was filmed with a fine mask of perspiration. She was both afraid and exhilarated. Attracted and repelled. For a moment she was twenty all over again.

Hot summer nights . . . hot skin . . . hot hands . . . hot bodies . . . But wait! Bradley had been the result of one of those hot summer nights. And right now Bradley was on the other side of the door. The thought cooled things down considerably.

She turned to Jeffrey, who was busy loosening his tie and undoing the top button on his shirt, whether from the heat or for expedience she wasn't sure. "Jeffrey, my son is staying with me. I don't think . . ."

Jeffrey, who was breathing a little easier now that the first wave of lust had crashed over him, summed up the situation immediately. Mother, son, son goes to bed, mother stays up. It was really very simple.

He leaned close to Maxine and let his eyes wander tenderly and expectantly over her face for a second before he spoke. "I'd like to meet him. Why don't you invite me in for a little nightcap?"

Maxine was still flustered. All sorts of long-forgotten feelings were racing around inside her. Part of her wanted him to come in and part of her wanted him to go away. And part of her—the practical part— was wondering if maybe she should reapply her lipstick before she went in to face her son, or if that would really give the game away. Her mother always knew when she had been kissed if she came home from a date with fresh lipstick. Would her son know it too?

"I—I don't think it's such a good idea. It's late, and . . ."

But Jeffrey was persistent. There was a lot at stake here. "It's only a little after ten," he coaxed, looking now the harmless, boyish young man from advertising and not the lascivious, lust-drenched demon lover of a few moments before.

Maxine felt herself begin to capitulate. *Maybe* it had been her fault. *Maybe* she had led him on. "I only have tap water."

Jeffrey knew he was well on his way to third base. "How about tea?"

"Tea?" That sounded so benign. A nice cup of tea. A little chit-chat with her son and good night and thank you for a lovely evening. It was the civilized thing to do. And there was absolutely nothing even remotely passionate about a cup of tea.

Exhaling with relief at not having to face the demons of her own sexuality, never mind Jeffrey's, Maxine unlocked the door and went into the apartment. Jeffrey followed and locked the door behind him. It was Little Maxine Riding Hood and the Wolf all over again.

"Bradley," called Maxine, but not too loudly in case she woke the baby. "Bradleeeey." This time a little louder. There was no answer. She turned to Jeffrey. "He must be in bed already. I'll just go and check." She started down the hall toward the bedrooms.

Jeffrey, the consummate seducer, noted the direction of his ulti-mate destination and then made himself comfortable on the couch. He was beginning to feel pretty good. He had been right about Maxine. A regular little firecracker. And not only that, but a firecracker that hadn't had its fuse lit in quite some time. It was going to be a long night. And he was looking forward to it.

A minute or two later she returned. Her face was pale and creased with worry. "They're not here."

"Maybe he took the baby out for a while. You know, visit some friends." Jeffrey shrugged. An empty apartment was even better than a son in bed. "Here, come and sit by me." He patted the couch next to his thigh.

But Maxine wasn't paying any attention. "I can't believe he'd take the baby out at this time of night. Something must have happened." She sounded fearful now, already anticipating the worst.

Jeffrey felt the moment slipping away. Nothing killed passion faster than fear. He stood up and went over to her, slipping a comforting arm around her shoulders and letting his hand dangle just above the heaving swell of her right breast.

"He's a big boy, Maxine. He's probably just gone out to get something for the baby and he took the kid because he didn't want to leave it alone in the apartment. He'll probably be right back." But as he said this he crossed the fingers on his other hand. The last thing he wanted at this point was any interruption.

"Do you really think so?" She sounded hopeful but unconvinced.

"I'm sure of it." He made his voice sound casual and relaxed and very matter-of-fact. "Now how about that tea?"

"Tea? Oh, yes."

As he suspected, the mention of tea distracted her sufficiently that she stopped dithering in the living room and went into the kitchen to put the water on. He congratulated himself silently as he followed her. Women were so easy to control. You just had to distract them enough so that they didn't know what was happening until it happened.

Maxine was getting two cups out of the cupboard and as she reached up to get them Jeffrey moved in for the kill. Quickly, and with a surefootedness that would have surprised a Balinese dancer, he grabbed her, kissed her, picked her up and started to carry her toward the bedroom, making sure he kept his mouth plastered to hers to stifle any protestations until he got her right where he wanted her. On the bed.

Shocked and more than a little overwhelmed at being manhandled in her own kitchen, Maxine didn't put up any resistance until she was halfway down the hall to the bedroom. Then she tore her mouth away from the sucking leeches of his lips. "What do you think you're doing?"

She kicked, trying to get free, but he was stronger and younger and more determined than she, and he held her tight against his chest and kicked open the door to her bedroom with one light tap of his foot.

"I want you, baby," he murmured, carrying her over to the bed. "I want you so bad."

Suddenly Maxine felt herself being catapulted out of his arms, through the air and onto the bedspread. Alone at last. But not for long. In a second he was beside her, one hand working itself up under her dress, the other pinning her shoulders to the coverlet.

"Jeffrey, get off me!" She struggled, devoid of passion now and filled with annoyance. She clamped her legs together as his fingers tried to infiltrate their way up the last few inches of Night Nude. "Jeffrey, please!"

But Jeffrey wasn't paying any attention. Somehow, while holding her, he had managed to work himself out of his jacket, undo his shirt and pull down the top of her dress and her bra strap so that one soft pale breast was bare to his touch. He seemed for a moment to possess more arms than Shiva and more lips than an octopus has suckers. He was all over her.

Maxine had the hysterical impression that there was more than one pushy young advertising executive wrestling with her on the bed. There was a whole conference room full!

"Jeffrey, I don't want to—Stop that!—*No!*"

He was kissing her neck, arms, face, breast. Then he whispered something in her ear.

"You want to do what?"

Five minutes on a bed with Jeffrey Mondavi had exposed Maxine to more sex education than twenty-five years of marriage. He was suggesting things that even Kinsey had never heard of, things that had never been written about to Dear Maxine. In another time, another situation, she would have taken notes. But at the moment both hands were busy fending off the salacious, squirming presence of Jeffrey Mondavi.

He tried again to get his hand up under her dress. He knew if he could just get the panty hose down she would stop pretending she didn't want what he wanted and they could get on with enjoying themselves.

He had managed to get his hand almost up to the waistband when all of a sudden he felt the impact of one stockinged knee right below his rib cage. For a moment he thought he was going to lose consciousness as his diaphragm deflated, driving all the oxygen out of his lungs.

As the strength ebbed from him, he released the grip on his hostess, and Maxine took the opportunity to slide off the far side of the bed. She landed *thump!* on the floor. But in a couple of seconds she was back on her feet, dress down, bra strap up, and kneeling on the bed.

"Are you all right?" She slapped him lightly on both sides of the face.

Jeffrey was gulping air, trying to reinflate his lungs, so he could not answer for the moment. And Maxine, whose emotions were already stretched as taut as a size-six knit on Tammy Bakker, was suddenly struck with a surge of hysteria.

She felt a wave of panic welling up inside her. "Oh my God! Oh my God!" she cried, her life flashing before her eyes as Jeffrey started to turn blue in the face. "My second date in twenty-five years and I killed him!" What would she tell Harry? What would she tell Bradley when he came home with the baby? The diapers are in the bedroom, dear, next to the dead man? She could see it now in the *Daily News.* "Grandmother Slays Boy Lover in Bed!" Her readers would have to write Dear Maxine care of Rikker's Island.

Jeffrey gave one pathetic little cough and then another. The color was gradually returning to his face. He drew in a deep, ragged breath and looked up at Maxine, who was still kneeling over him. "Boy, I know some women like to play rough, but you play too rough for me, baby."

He tried to sit up, but she pushed him down again. "Lie there. Breathe. In. Out. In . . . That's it."

In a few minutes he was fully recovered. He sat up. "Well, I can't say it hasn't been fun."

Cured of her fear now, Maxine felt her anger coming back. "What's wrong with you!"

"Me! What's wrong with *me*!"

"You tried to rape me," she accused, wagging a finger under his nose.

"I did not. You wanted it as much as I did."

"I did not!"

"Come on, Maxine, I know when a woman is responding to me, and you responded."

What could she say? He was right. To a point. She stood up and went out of the bedroom, down the hall and into the living room. In a few minutes, Jeffrey appeared. "Well, I guess it's *adios*, he said, straightening his tie.

Maxine continued to sit on the couch. She was thinking. There was a question that still had to be answered before she could officially file this evening under O for over.

Having decided that there were not going to be any lingering good-byes, Jeffrey started toward the door.

"Wait!" She got up and came after him.

"Change your mind?" he asked hopefully.

Maxine gave him a look that said "Not in this century!" And then she asked, "Why me?"

"What?"

"I said, why me? Why not any of those girls in the restaurant, any of the girls at the magazine? Why me?"

Jeffrey pulled on his coat and then turned to face her. "It's pretty simple, babe. You're safe."

"I'm what?"

"Safe."

"You mean you don't have to worry about me getting pregnant?"

Jeffrey gave a laugh that sounded more than a little like a snicker. "No, baby, that's your problem, not mine. What I mean is, you've been married for twenty-five years to the same guy. And you older broads never fucked around. So that makes you safe."

Maxine still had not got the message.

Jeffrey sighed and tried again. "I mean, I can't *catch* anything deadly from you. Get it?" And he unlocked the door and went out into the hall. "Let me know if you change your mind, O.K.? We could still make beautiful music. Catch ya later." And he was gone.

Bradley came home a few minutes later. Maxine was sitting in the living room mulling things over. She had attributed many motives to Jeffrey Mondavi and his attraction to her, but *safety* had never been one of them. And she didn't much care for being called an "older broad." But what was really troubling her—aside from the fact that she was almost a date rape statistic, and that she could partly forgive because when it came right down to it, for a moment or three she had actually wanted him to—was the fact that she had once judged potential dates by the width of their shoulders, the curliness of their hair and the color of their eyes. This element of *safety* was a whole new consideration. It was just too much!

"Hi, Ma," said Bradley a little sheepishly as he came into the living room.

Maxine looked up from her musings. Immediately something struck her as not quite right. He was on his own. Sans baby.

"Where's—"

"At the hospital."

"The hospital!" Maxine clutched one hand with the other and then moved both hands up to her throat. This evening was turning into one of her worst nightmares. "I knew it. I should have stayed home. I shouldn't have gone out—in more ways than one. What happened?"

"Take it easy, Ma. He's O.K. Bradley sat beside her and patted her shoulder with a soothing hand. "He just had a temperature, that's all. I took him to the hospital because I didn't know what else to do. The doctor said it's pretty normal for small babies to get temperatures and that there's nothing to worry about. They're just going to keep him in overnight for observation."

Maxine relaxed a little. Just a temperature. That was a relief. For a moment she was afraid that Bradley had done something like drop the baby on his head. It had been that kind of an evening.

"Only overnight? All right, I'll pick him up on the way to work in the morning." She was glad to get back to what passed for normal in her life.

"No, Ma, that's O.K. I'll go and get him."

Maxine looked at her son in surprise. Something had transpired between him and his son while she was fending off the lascivious Jeffrey. Something that looked remarkably like parenthood. "All right, if you think you can handle him while I'm at work."

"No problem, Ma." Bradley got up. "You want a cup of tea?"

"No! No tea. I mean I'm tired. I think I'll just go to bed."

She got up and started down the hall to her room.

He called after her. "Ma?"

"What?"

"When I thought the baby was really sick tonight, I was scared and then I felt . . ." He searched for the appropriate words, and then shrugged. "Oh, I dunno."

Maxine smiled to herself. She knew what he was trying to say even if he didn't. "I know."

Bradley grinned. "Yeah, I guess you do. And you know what else?"

Maxine shook her head.

"I kind of liked the idea that he needed me, you know, really needed me. I was important to him."

"It's one of the perks," said Maxine softly, though she had a little trouble getting the words out because a lump had started to rise in her throat. *Her* baby was finally growing up.

"Good night, Ma."

"Good night, son."

CHAPTER THIRTEEN

CHESTER WAS WAGGLE-WALKING across the back of the sofa, digging his long curved toenails into the fabric and using his fan of tail feathers for balance. And balance was an issue of prime importance, because keeping pace beneath him was a large, threatening white mass that was setting all his bird nerves on edge.

The parrot rolled his orange eyes and flexed his wings, once, twice, in a display of birdly bravado, and then negotiated his way carefully around Janie's shoulders. He looked down once more. The interloper was still there. At least, thought Chester to himself, when Bradley used to come over, he came alone. This new man, however, came with reinforcements.

Anxiously looking up at the tiny feathered figure, Tony was a seething mass of quivering canine instincts. From the tense flexing of his nostrils, to the tingling in the taut tips of his whiskers, to the throbbing of blood in every vein and capillary of his little dog's body, one perception was being flashed along the wire bundles of his nerves, assaulting his brain with its primeval possibilities. That perception was *bird*.

After a few more moments, his brain, stirred from centuries of domesticated lethargy, finally managed to convert the perception into a reality that was a little more meaningful, a reality that exploded from his primal memory like a grenade—*food*. And Tony, true to the instincts of his ancestors, responded accordingly. He launched himself straight up like a helicopter, jaws open and ready, tongue soaked with saliva, taste buds oozing and waiting for the flavor of *bird*.

But fortunately, Chester saw him coming and with one petrified squawk he catapulted off the back of the couch, took one daringly dangerous swoop toward the white mass, and then glided up to the top of the bookcase with a triumphant cackle and began to plot his revenge.

"Cut that out, Tony!" cried Steve, taking a swipe at the dog, who ducked under the coffee table just in time. Then he turned to Janie. "Sorry about that. I guess he's just not used to birds."

"That's O.K. He's only following his instincts. And anyway, I think Chester was taunting him. He's very territorial about his space." She yawned a little and continued to sit half slumped against the back of the couch, legs stretched out in front of her, a cup of cappuccino balancing warmly on her stomach. She was suspended in a delicious Friday-night, end-of-the-week lethargy and she was glad to have someone to share it with.

"So when did you say Lavinia was coming back?"

"End of next week, I think. This has been a long trip." He drained the last of the cappuccino from his cup and set it back on the table. "You know, I think that she thinks that if she stays away long enough I'll miss her enough to ask her to marry me."

"And what do you think?"

"I think she knows me pretty well." Steve settled back on the couch. He was also feeling pleasantly content and relaxed, not to mention full, after the dinner Janie had cooked for the two of them. This domestic life wasn't bad after all.

"I never knew you were such a good cook."

"I'm not. It was more luck than anything else."

"I doubt that. You're not the type of woman who leaves anything to luck."

Janie decided to acknowledge the compliment. "Well, I've had a lot of time on my hands lately . . . You know, when Bradley was here

I never used to find the time to cook for us, but now that I'm on my own . . . It's kind of funny, isn't it? I mean, it's supposed to be the other way around." The look on her face said that she wanted him to say something to absolve her from her domestic guilt. The guilt of not looking after the man while she had him. But being a man and totally unaware of the rise of this recent female dilemma, he interpreted the look in his own way.

"You miss him, don't you?" Steve reached out a comforting hand. Janie took it and nodded. "Why don't you call him?"

"I can't. I told you, I'm not about to raise another woman's child. It may sound cruel but I know how I feel. Believe me, it wouldn't be fair to me—and even worse, it wouldn't be fair to the child."

But Steve, who couldn't understand how anyone could look a gift baby in the face, persevered. "Maybe it's just that you've never spent any time with kids. They're not that much different from animals, you know." As he said this he patted the recalcitrant Tony, who had crept up beside him on the couch. "Animals aren't related by blood, and yet we love them, we care for them."

Janie was a long way from being convinced. "You can say that because you've got kids of your own. How would you feel about raising a child who wasn't yours?"

"I think I could handle it. I guess."

"All right then, what about this? What if Lavinia had a child by another man? Would you still want to raise it?"

Steve thought for a moment. This was a subject he had never given much consideration to, partly because the possibility of Lavinia having a child by another man was so remote. After all, she wouldn't even consider having one with him. He knew that because he had asked her often enough, but she always said her career came first. All the same, he answered Janie's question in the affirmative.

"You're just saying that because you're trying to get me to see things your way. It's very easy for you to have an opinion when your children were both born in a normal old-fashioned marriage. Bradley didn't even *know* this woman. She could be—" Janie sought for an appropriately awful possibility, couldn't come up with one that struck the right note and so settled for "weird. No, strike the *could*. I know she must be weird. I caught a glimpse of her at the synagogue. She had pink hair! You know what that means?"

Steve shrugged. "She likes pastels?"

Janie refused to be put off. "She named the baby *Rogue!*"

"So she has bad taste in names."

"You just don't understand, do you? It's like, like . . . O.K., how about this? If you could have a choice between a dog with a pedigree like Tony or one from the pound, which one would you pick?"

"It's not the same thing," countered Steve, although he wasn't sure he was a hundred percent right. After all, he *had* gone out of his way to get Tony from a reputable breeder.

"It's exactly the same thing," argued Janie.

"You mean the reason you don't want to raise this baby is because you don't know its blood lines?"

When he put it that way it sounded kind of silly, but Janie wasn't about to back down. "That's part of it," she replied defensively.

"So then if Bradley had had an affair and had a child with a woman he knew and cared for, then you might consider . . . ?"

Janie shook her head vehemently. "Oh no. Uh-uh. No way. I don't need a lifetime reminder of misspent passion running around the house."

"So what you're saying, then, is that you don't want to raise the baby because you don't know who its mother was, but if you *did* know who its mother was, you wouldn't want to raise it either?"

"I told you, you just don't understand." She folded her arms across her chest and fell silent.

Steve sat quietly for a few moments and then he made a decision. "Look, I'm going to tell you something now that I've never told anyone else. Not even Lavinia. Especially not Lavinia."

Janie was surprised by the urgency in his voice. She had the distinct impression that their conversation had shifted from the philosophical to the practical.

Steve cleared his throat. "I told you how much I missed my kids after the divorce?"

Janie nodded.

"Well, it got so bad . . . I wanted to be a father again so much that I decided I would have another baby."

"What?"

Steve nodded. "I decided I would pay a woman to have my baby for me. I even went so far as to make all the arrangements. I went to a doctor who specializes in this sort of thing and he found me a woman who was willing to do it for $10,000 plus expenses."

Janie was intrigued. "So what happened?"

"I changed my mind."

"Why?"

"It was during the time that there was all that fuss about surrogate mothers who wanted to keep the babies after they were born. Remember the Baby M case and all the others? So I thought, what if the surrogate who is having my baby decides she wants to keep it? I just couldn't face losing custody of another one of my children, so I called it off."

Now it was Janie's turn to offer comfort. "I'm sorry." She paused. "Kind of a crazy situation we have here, isn't it? I mean, there you are wishing you had a baby and here I am wishing Bradley didn't."

Steve nodded. "Yeah, life can be a pretty strange business. I guess that's why it pays not to think about it too much." He hesitated then, reflecting for a moment on the inequities of existence, found that he was making himself depressed and decided to snap out of it while he still could. "I guess what I'm trying to say is, maybe you shouldn't think so much about who the mother was. It's the baby that counts. Some people would give a lot to be in your shoes."

"Well, I'm not one of them."

The discussion ground to a halt. But after another few minutes of silence broken only by the soft swishing of feathers as Chester stretched and flexed his wings, Steve broke the silence. "Hey, you want to see some pictures of my kids?"

"Sure," replied Janie, though she had a distinct feeling that he had something a little more up his sleeve than simply displaying his offspring.

Steve had his wallet out and open on the table in less than two blinks of an eye. He spread several photographs out in front of Janie. "These are recent. This is Bethany." He pointed to the picture of a pretty little girl whose childish charm was spoiled only by the hard set of her mouth. Fortunately, thought Janie, it was not the sort of thing a father was likely to notice. At least not at this age. Next to that was a picture of a boy of about twelve or thirteen, who Janie knew without a doubt was Jared. He was the spitting image of his father, though in a skinny preadolescent, rather unfinished way.

Janie admired the pictures at length and then Steve presented several others of the children at various ages. She dipped deep into her bag of adjectives to find the appropriate comments, noticing as she commented on each one that all of the photographs were well handled.

"And now I'm saving the best for last. These"—he pulled out two small pictures from another section of the wallet—"are pictures of them when they were babies. The one with the blond hair is Bethany, of course, and the other one is my son."

Janie carefully took the well-worn photographs. Neither child had changed much between these and the later photos, and Jared even as a baby was undoubtedly his father's child, right down to the thick crop of black hair, though without the gray, of course.

"They're lovely," she said, handing back the pictures. "I'm sure you must be very proud of them."

"Yeah," replied Steve. "And they're not only cute, they're smart as hell." He paused. "You know something? Tomorrow's my custody visit. Why don't you come along? I'm taking the kids to the zoo. We'll have some fun. I know you'll love them. And maybe," he shrugged, "who knows, if you can like my kids, enjoy being with them, then you might want to give some more thought to how you feel about Bradley's kid. Whaddaya say?"

"I don't think—"

But before she could get out even half the sentence, Chester took a maniacal kamikaze-like dive down from the top of the bookcase directly at the unsuspecting Tony, who was busy lapping from a bowl of water that Janie had conveniently placed by the kitchen door. With a silent swoosh of feathers he zeroed in on his furry white nemesis like an air-to-dog heat-seeking missile.

It was all over so fast that all Tony saw was a flash of mean green, and then he felt a searing pain at the back of his neck as the impact of the bird-warrior knocked him off balance and sent him face first into the water bowl. Chester, his mission accomplished, soared once more up to his belletristic aerie, clutching a silken tuft of white hair in his beak.

"Chester!" cried Janie, wagging a threatening finger at him. "One more incident like that and you're dead poultry. Understand?"

Chester, imperious with victory, only puffed out his feathers.

Steve was comforting the shivering, slightly hysterical Tony, who had sequestered himself under the couch out of beak's way. When he was sure the dog was all right he repeated his question to Janie.

She thought for a minute, decided that, after all, to say no would be to risk hurting Steve's feelings, and said yes. And anyway, it wasn't as though she had anything else to do on Saturday.

Even the best of intentions can result in the worst of experiences. It would not be stretching the bounds of credibility to say that Janie's day with Steve and his children could be summed up in two words—Dis-aster.

It all began benignly enough when Steve picked up Janie and the two of them headed for Grand Central Station to meet the train bearing Steve's progeny in from suburbia. Steve was in the best mood Janie had ever seen him in, a state she attributed rightly enough to the fact that he was about to have a whole day with his kids. They were running a little late, and rather than risk having little Bethany and Jared detraining and finding no one to meet them, Steve decided they should grab a cab. He flagged one down and he and Janie hopped into the back seat.

"Grand Central Station and step on it," he called to the driver and then turned to Janie. "I've always wanted to say that." He laughed. And, good moods being catching, Janie laughed with him. The driver just turned on the meter. He had heard it all before—several hundred times.

When they got into the station, the nine o'clock train from Fairfield was just pulling in. "Perfect timing," cried Steve, grabbing Janie's hand and hurrying along the platform. But fifteen minutes later they were sitting on a bench without the children, drinking bitter coffee from styrofoam cups. Steve's mood had deflated somewhat and Janie was silent, letting him deal with what she guessed must be either anger or frustration.

After a few minutes he heaved an enormous sigh. "Wouldn't you think that considering I only get the kids once every three weeks *she* could get her ass out of bed in time to get them to the station to catch the goddamn train? She's doing this on purpose, I know she is."

Janie tried to placate him. "Everybody misses trains from time to time. Don't let it spoil the day. She told you when you called that she had put them on the ten o'clock train. They'll be here"—she checked her watch—"in another forty-five minutes." She smiled. "I'm really looking forward to meeting them."

Steve glowered for another minute or two and then crushed the styrofoam cup in one hand and flipped it into a nearby garbage container. And as if he was tossing out the bad feelings along with the used container, he turned to Janie and smiled. "You're right. There's no point letting her spoil the whole day. Anyway, it's probably just what she wants." He looked around the station. "You want to play some video games or look at the magazine stand while we wait?"

Forty-five minutes later the next train pulled in, and Janie breathed a sigh of relief when she saw Steve's face light up.

"There they are!" he cried, and he rushed up the platform to meet them. Janie hung back, deciding that it would be better for him to see his kids alone first. She saw him hug and kiss both children enthusiastically. And they in turn grudgingly allowed themselves to be hugged and kissed. Then he turned and pointed at Janie and began to herd the children in her direction. This gave Janie an opportunity to form a first impression from a distance.

Bethany was all pink skin, blue eyes and blond hair, a vision of Tinkerbell in acid-washed denim. And Jared was long and stringy with the enormous hands and feet of a body that was still playing catch-up with its own growth. And as if to prove that, he walked with all the awkward grace of someone whose legs seem to have grown longer overnight. They were very attractive children.

"Janie," said Steve happily, "this is Jared and this is Bethany."

Janie formed a wide, nonthreatening smile and beamed down at both children. "Hello, I'm so—"

Tinkerbell interrupted. "Who's *she*?" she said to her father, curling her rosebud lips into a childish sneer.

"Uh . . ." Steve looked over at Janie, his eyes begging for patience. "Janie is a friend of mine."

"Oh? What happened to Lavinia?" It sounded more like an accusation than simple curiosity.

But before Steve could answer, Jared, bored with picking at the pimple in the middle of his chin, joined in. "He probably dumped her. Mom said she wouldn't last."

"Lavinia is on a buying trip to Europe," said Steve firmly, and then to round out the explanation, "Janie and I are just friends."

"I'll bet," said Tinkerbell, wrinkling up her nose and looking at Janie with the eyes of a thirty-six-year-old divorced mother of two.

Janie who had never met children as openly hostile as these, was momentarily at a loss as to what to do. Her immediate reaction was to bail out of this little outing and salvage what was left of her Saturday in the soothing and comfortable presence of the devoted Chester. But, nasty little children not withstanding, she knew she had a responsibility to Steve to try to stick it out.

For his part, Steve was used to his children acting like this. They had been doing it ever since before the divorce. At first he had put it down to the trauma of being a part of a disintegrating family and so had tried to be patient, loving and understanding at their little outbursts. Later, of course, as their behavior failed to improve and in fact got worse, he put it down to their having to adjust to their mother's new marriage and their new stepfather, Bubba. And lately he had begun to ascribe it to the fact that Jared was teetering on the brink of puberty and so would naturally be prone to less than civilized behavior. Any or all of the above were preferable to having to face the truth. And so he put on a big smile and said, "Guess where we're going today?"

The children just looked bored.

"We're going to the zoo!" cried Steve excitedly.

"The zoo?" they whined in unison. "That's kid stuff."

"We wanna go to Times Square," said little Bethany.

"Yeah, who wants to go see a bunch of dumb animals. We wanna see the pimps and the hookers and the drug addicts," added Jared gleefully. "Just like on TV."

Steve shook his head with a little chuckle. "It's the zoo today, I'm afraid." And he began to lead them all toward the exit.

As they went through the revolving doors, Janie couldn't help herself. She leaned close to Steve and whispered, "Don't they have PBS in Fairfield?"

Two hours later they had "done" the Central Park Zoo. And not surprisingly the only ones who enjoyed the exhibits were Steve and Janie. The children had remained bored throughout—that is when they weren't arguing with each other.

"You pushed me," cried Bethany.

"Did not," lied Jared, pushing her again.

"Did too," wailed Bethany and shoved him back.

Janie had spent the entire two hours trying to pretend that she was not with these children just in case she ran into anyone she knew, or even worse, in case anyone should think that she was their mother. This was not as difficult as it sounded, because neither of them had said a word to her since leaving the train station.

Steve meanwhile had been busy wiping noses, refereeing bouts of pushing, shoving and whining and stuffing enough popcorn and candy apples into them to feed a small South American country, in an effort to be a loving, understanding and sympathetic divorced father. It was only to be expected, therefore, that as they finished their tour of the zoo, Jared, after a brief consultation with Bethany, turned to Steve and complained, "We're hungry."

And Steve, like any other deposed daddy, had already planned for that eventuality. "Good, we're all having lunch at the Palm Court."

"The Palm Court! But we wanna go to McDonald's," cried Bethany, her steel-blue eyes welling with tears at the possibility of not getting her own way.

Patiently, Steve hunkered down in front of his daughter so he could talk to her face to face. "Bethany, honey, you can go to McDonald's any time. This is a special lunch and we want to have it in a special place. Don't we? Besides, we want Janie to enjoy her lunch, and I don't think she would like McDonald's as much as the Palm Court." His voice was full of soft fatherly reason.

Bethany sniffed back a few tears. "Who cares what *she* wants."

"I do," said Steve, standing up again and looking over at Janie. "Because I invited her."

Lunch was no picnic. The children didn't want anything on the menu, and it was only when Steve finally allowed that they could select anything they wanted from the dessert table instead that any kind of goodwill was established. Even then, Jared sat sullenly in his seat because Steve wouldn't let him have a sip from his glass of beer. "Bubba always lets me," he said before clamming up entirely.

When it was almost over, and Janie was thinking that this was possibly the longest morning and afternoon she had ever had to endure, Bethany leaned over and whispered something to her father. Steve nodded and then turned to Janie. "Would you mind taking her to the ladies' room?"

Glad for any excuse to get away from the table and hurry the afternoon along to a grateful conclusion, Janie was on her feet in a flash. "Not at all." And she reached out to take the little girl by the hand.

But Bethany ignored the proffered hand. "I can go by myself," she said to Steve.

Janie shrugged and walked toward the washrooms. She knew Bethany was following her because she could see her reflection as they passed the store windows that lined the hallway leading to the lower level.

A few minutes later, standing in front of adjoining sinks, the little girl looked up at the mirror and caught Janie's reflection. "I don't like you," she said with as much venom as an eight-year-old could manage.

"Is that so?" replied Janie as she calmly finished washing her hands. "Well, I don't like you either." And then she left the little girl standing at the sink.

Bethany quickly dried her hands and followed Janie out into the hall. When they got back to the table, Steve was paying the bill.

"Janie says she doesn't like me," simpered Bethany to her father as soon as she sat down.

Steve threw a questioning look at Janie, who shrugged. "She said it first."

Steve turned to his daughter. "Janie's my friend. So I'm sure you didn't mean what you said, did you Bethany, honey?"

Bethany-honey pulled a face and then answered, "Yes, I did. She's not your *friend*. She's just another one of your women. Just like Momma said." And then she looked at Janie and poked a tiny little tip of tongue between the soft pink blossoms of her lips.

"I'm sorry," said Steve to Janie. "She's not comfortable around strangers."

"No, just pimps, hookers and drug addicts," replied Janie acidly. She was upset with herself because this child, this Tinkerbell terrorist, was making *her* feel like she shouldn't be there.

With forced jocularity Steve tried to rescue the moment. "Well, enough of that. Now, what do you two want to do this afternoon?"

Jared, roused from his sulk by the question, looked at his Mickey Mouse watch. "It's three-thirty. We have to meet Mom and Daddy-Bubba at four o'clock."

"What!" cried Steve in disbelief. "You're supposed to have the whole day with me."

Bethany chimed in then. "Bubba's taking us to the Christmas Show at Radio City and then we're going skating at Rockefeller Center."

Steve slumped slightly in his chair and looked at Janie. "I guess Brenda strikes again," he sighed, a man defeated one more time by a woman he used to call "sugar-lips."

Janie knew it wasn't very nice, but for her part she felt relief flooding through her body at the thought that her day with Steve's children was fast approaching its finale. She was tired, she was fed-up, and most of all she was disillusioned. Somewhere in the back of her mind she had envisioned that the day might lead to a revelation. A new appreciation for the children of her species. Perhaps even the germ of a growing fascination. But it was not to be. Not after a day with these kids.

She was sure now that she had made the right decision about Bradley and his baby. Sometimes it was hard enough to love your own children. She could see that from the look on Steve's face. To love someone else's children, therefore . . .

Later that afternoon, after they had delivered the children to Radio City Music Hall, Steve walked Janie back toward SOFI. They were quiet, companionable, keeping step in spite of the surging Christmas crowds. When they were almost there, Steve spoke up.

"My idea didn't work very well, did it?"

Janie shook her head.

"You know, they're not that bad, really. It's just that they're going through a stage what with the divorce and everything."

"I know," said Janie, who was not about to be the one to burst Steve's fatherly fantasies. He was having enough trouble keeping them intact as it was. "You want to come in for a drink?"

"No, I think I'll pass." He stuffed both hands into the depths of his pockets. "Anyway, I gotta get home and take Tony out. You know, I really miss him when I haven't seen him all day. And he's always so glad to see me." He turned and walked back up the street and into the gathering winter dusk.

CHAPTER FOURTEEN

THE DAY AFTER BRADLEY PICKED ROGUE UP from the hospital he decided to tell Maxine the full extent of his experience with Nurse McAdams. Now that he knew the baby was O.K. and his own parental panic had subsided, he was able to appreciate the funny side of things. Imagine not being able to answer even the simplest of questions about your own baby! The old nurse must have thought he was a pretty weird kind of a father, all right. But then, come to think of it, he *was* a pretty weird kind of a father. So he told his mother the whole story with plenty of emphasis and a few embellishments here and there to get the maximum impact.

Maxine, whose own sense of humor fortunately ran to the bizarre, and sometimes even past it, thought the part about her being Rogue's mother was funny enough, and Bradley's description of Nurse McAdams looking over her glasses and saying "And what is *in* the bottle, Mr. Kraft" drew a bout of appreciative laughter. But the other part—the part about Bradley not knowing what could have been life or death information about his son—was not funny at all. She knew something had to be done to rectify that situation and the sooner the better.

"We'll have to find the mother," she said to Bradley. "We need to know a few things about the baby in case this ever happens again. And also, one of these days you're going to need a birth certificate to enroll him in school, so we need to get that from her too."

"School!" cried Bradley, who had no desire to see the woman with the pink hair again, especially not up close. "He's only a few months old, Ma. We don't have to worry about school just yet."

"*You* were only a few months old once, and now look at you. Time passes. Believe me, we need the birth certificate." It was not a justification—it was a determination. And Bradley knew that when his mother used that tone of voice there was no point in arguing with her. Determination, however, could not necessarily overcome situation. The one thing in his favor and against Maxine's plan was that they had no idea who or where Rogue's mother was. Or at least, that's what he thought.

"O.K., Ma," he agreed, taking a conciliatory stance before trying to dissuade her with logic. "But how are we going to do that? We don't even know who the mother is. She may not even be in Manhattan anymore. She could be . . ." He swept his arms in a wide arc to show the absolute impossibility of their situation, "anywhere."

"With pink hair? Where else is she going to go? Des Moines?" Maxine retorted with a logic of her own.

"All right." Bradley nodded in agreement. He felt it was safe to concede the "where" issue. "But, Ma, even if she's still in New York, even if she's still on the island, do you know how many women there are in Manhattan with pink hair?"

"Too many," replied Maxine and went to get her purse. When she returned she took out her wallet, opened it and extracted a folded slip of blue paper. "But there can't be too many whose names are"—she consulted the American Express receipt—"Pauline McCormick."

"What!" cried Bradley, almost leaping across the space that separated them. "Where did you get that?"

Maxine shrugged. "It was in the bottom of the bag that the baby came in. I kept it because I thought one day it might come in handy."

Bradley was still in a mild case of shock. The woman with the pink hair, the mother of his son, had a name *and* an American Express card. He could see it now. One of these days he was going to switch on the television set and there she would be—

"Hi, you don't know me, but I'm the mother of Rogue Kraft. I may have given up my baby, but I never go anywhere without my American Express card."

Oh God!

Rogue had a mother. A woman who owed money, had an address and a life! She was a real person, not just a nameless, incorporeal womb from which had erupted the tiny, perfect body of his son. It was an idea that even in the raw stages of its development had far-reaching implications. Not the least of which was the possibility that at some point she might change her mind and conclude that the contribution of an egg makes for a better parent than the contribution of a sperm and decide she wanted her *baby back*. The baby that he had come to think of as solely his—and Maxine's, of course.

"Ma, I don't think we should go looking for her. She could cause problems. You know." Bradley wasn't sure how to put his fatherly feelings into words. They were still embryonic and he wasn't yet used to feeling them. But the overwhelming specter of Rogue having another parent out there who might also want him was filling him with dread.

Maxine, ever practical, knew that a situation once arisen has to be confronted. "We have to do it for the sake of the baby," she said gently. "Think about it. One of these days, twenty years from now, he's going to walk into a bar—no, make that a library—meet a girl, and when she asks him what sign he was born under, what's he going to say, Bloomingdale's?"

Bradley knew she was right. He couldn't go on pretending that his son didn't have a mother, especially when the woman had information that would be vital to his child's life. "I guess you're right, Ma," he agreed reluctantly. "But how do we find out where this Pauline McCormick lives?"

"We look her up in the phone book," replied Maxine with excruciating simplicity, and went to get one.

There were several listings for McCormick, P. It was Bradley who picked out the most likely one.

"That's her," he said to Maxine, running his finger below the name. "How can you be so sure?"

"It's in Tribeca, Ma. That's definitely a pink hair area."

Maxine thought that sounded reasonable enough. After all, Bradley had gone through a few hair colors himself when he was younger, so he would know about these things.

"Do you think we should call her?" he asked, his heart pounding, trepidation trickling through his veins like so much liquid amphetamine.

Maxine thought for a moment. "No, I think this requires a visit."

"When do you think we should go and see her?" Bradley was thinking maybe next week or the week after. Sometime in the sweet by-and-by. Any time, in fact, except right now.

"Now," replied Maxine, and before he could protest she was on her way to get her coat.

It all happened so fast that he and Maxine and the baby were standing outside the door of Joyce and Harry's apartment before he knew where they were going.

Joyce opened the door.

"You're sure you don't mind?" asked Bradley's mother, passing his son over to his stepmother.

"Like I said on the phone, it's no problem," replied Joyce, receiving the baby and settling him in the curve of her arm.

"It'll only be for a couple of hours," said Maxine. "Bradley and I have a little errand to run."

"Fine. Take your time," replied Joyce. "Rogue and I know how to get along. Don't we, baby?" Her voice went up a decibel or two and she pulled a funny face as she looked down at the scrunched up pink face in the blanket.

As they waited for the elevator to take them back downstairs, Bradley remarked to his mother that Joyce seemed to be putting on a little weight.

"That's married life," explained Maxine matter-of-factly, though she didn't say *which* particular part of married life was responsible for Joyce's expanding waistline. She had already decided that if Joyce and Harry were going to go ahead with the pregnancy—and it looked as though they were—it was Harry's job to tell his son he was about to become a brother, not hers.

They took a cab down Seventh Avenue, past Houston Street and on down to Canal and lower, descending farther and farther into the lower reaches of the island. Maxine had never been "down here" before. It was a part of Manhattan that nice Jewish girls of her generation avoided for the simple reason that there was nothing here to attract them. And, reflected Maxine as she stared out the window of the taxi at the ever-deteriorating view, if there was nothing there to attract them when they were young, there was even less when they got older. Or to put it another way, it was a lo-o-o-ong walk to Saks.

Finally, after hitting his thirty-second pothole of the journey—Maxine knew this because she had kept track—the driver let them off at the foot of Thomas Street.

Maxine got out of the cab, looked around and clutched her purse just a little more tightly under her left arm. With her other hand she grabbed hold of her son. In her mind there were all sorts of dubious lifeforms lurking in the alleys and the doorways they would have to pass to reach their destination. And she wasn't about to take any chances. She wanted to survive her visit to New York's netherworld with both kid and credit cards intact.

"Definitely a pink hair area," she said to her son. And then, screwing up her courage, "Come on." She started off down the street in the direction of what looked like a group of decrepit warehouses.

When they got to the right one, or rather the one with the right address, since none of these buildings could have been described as being even remotely "right" in any other sense of the word, Maxine took a deep breath, and being careful to keep her gloves on, cautiously reached up a finger and pushed a buzzer that looked like it had already been the victim of several thousand ungloved and grimy hands.

Bradley hung back, still unconvinced that this was the right or even the safe thing to do.

"Maybe nobody's home," he urged hopefully, tugging at his mother's arm as she went to push the buzzer one more time.

But before she could reach it, a voice crackled over the intercom. "Who's there?"

"It's Maxine Kraft," said Maxine, leaning close to the intercom but being careful not to inhale just in case any germs were lingering from whomever had last leaned this way.

There was a pause before the voice responded with a guarded, "So?"

This threw Maxine for a second. "My son and I would like to talk to you."

Again there was a pause. "What about?" asked the voice with more than a hint of suspicion.

"Ah . . . It's about Rogue." It was the first time Maxine had willingly said the name out loud, and she made the sacrifice only now for the sake of expediency. If whoever was on the other end of the intercom knew anything about a certain baby, then this was the way to establish their connection. If not, then it was better to establish that now, while they were still outside and capable of beating a hasty retreat.

But a few seconds later the bleat of the door buzzer signaled that the disembodied voice did indeed know someone named Rogue.

"Well, come on," said Maxine, sounding much braver than she felt. Anything could be on the other side of that door. Drug addicts, pimps, thieves, mice!

They went through the decaying, peeling door with its pollution-encrusted pane of glass, over the crumbling, sagging threshold and—into another world.

Maxine, though she may have suspected many things lay beyond the door, had not expected this hidden display of opulence. But she was not reassured. In fact, she was immediately on the alert.

"Look at this place," she whispered sotto voce to her son.

"Yeah, isn't it great!" cried Bradley, who had suddenly gained a whole new respect for the woman with the pink hair.

"Shush!" warned Maxine as they began to climb the stairs. She was sure now that there were videocameras and microphones hidden nearby to keep an eye on the comings and goings and whisperings of those who had witnessed the glories of this Manhattan version of Ali Baba's cave. "There's something wrong here."

"Wrong? What's wrong? This place is fantastic!"

"That's what's wrong. Fantastic places do not get hidden away inside derelict old warehouses. It defeats the point. Whoever owns this place is trying to hide something."

"Ma, come on. Maybe they just like it this way."

"Nobody in their right mind would like living this way in *this* area. If they like living this way, they should be living uptown where they can be in *Architectural Digest*. Unless they're up to something." She ran her hand over the expensive carved banister. "Drug money," she mouthed the words to her son and nodded once to reinforce her point.

"Oh, Ma . . ."

They reached the top of the stairs, and Maxine was beginning to wish that she had let Bradley talk her out of coming here after all. A simple telephone call would have been enough. And, if a meeting had been necessary, a nice crowded public place—say, the third floor of Lord and Taylor's during the pre-Christmas sale—would have been a much better choice than this.

Before they could even knock at the door at the top of the stairs, it opened with just enough of a creak that the hairs on Maxine's neck stood up in spite of her turtleneck sweater. And the hairs stayed at attention when she saw that standing a few steps inside the doorway was a tall, muscular woman with short-cropped black hair. She was wearing a man's white undershirt with the sleeves rolled up, a pair of black leather jeans, and cowboy boots with spurs.

"I have a feeling we're not in Kansas anymore," murmured Bradley.

"Shut up," hissed Maxine at the same time as she was smiling her hello to the woman with the spurs.

"Come in," said the woman. And without smiling back she moved aside so they could both enter.

Bradley and Maxine sidled past her into the luxe interior of the loft. Neither one of them had any idea who this woman was, but neither one of them was about to challenge her right to be there—or anywhere else, for that matter.

Maxine spoke first. "We are looking for Pauline McCormick," she said with more authority than she actually felt.

"Yeah," said the woman and turned and walked over to the area that evidently served as a living room. Maxine deduced this because although the loft contained no interior walls, the furniture was grouped in the traditional manner. A bed was paired with night tables further down the open space and here, couches and chairs were mixed in with coffee tables, speakers, guitars and keyboards.

"You're a musician!" cried Maxine, her voice displaying a note of relief because she could now account for both the location of the loft, the look of the woman and the luxury of the surroundings without having to ascribe criminal activity to any or all of the above—a circumstance that made her personal safety quotient soar to the highest level it had been since they had passed Herald Square.

"I know who I am. What I don't know is who you are," replied the woman aggressively as she took out a cigarette from the pack that had been rolled up in one short white sleeve.

"I'm Maxine Kraft, and this is my—"

"Yeah, we did that number already," Paulie let out half a dozen perfect smoke rings in quick succession. "What I meant was, *who* the hell are you and what's this got to do with Rogue?"

Maxine waved an errant smoke ring away from her face. "My son—Bradley—is the father of a baby named Rogue. We found an American Express receipt."

Paulie nodded. "Oh yeah? I get it. Luba left the receipt in the bag when she took the kid to the synagogue. So much for keeping it anonymous. Jeez!" Paulie shook her head in amazement. "You know, she may have looks. She may even have talent. But sometimes when I look at her I can see that even though the lights are on, there's nobody home. You know what I mean?" She took another deep drag on the cigarette and gave Bradley the once-over. "So you're the father, eh?" was all she said.

Bradley wasn't sure if he had just been insulted or not, and if he had been, what he planned to do about it since this woman looked like she could quite easily reduce him to a series of compound fractures without knocking the ash off the end of her cigarette. He decided not to pursue her opinion of his paternity.

Maxine picked up the slack. "He is the father, and Pauline McCormick is the mother. We'd like to see her. Is she in?"

"Yeah, she's in," said Paulie, who was beginning to enjoy her little game of cat and mouse with these two, who looked so straight they could be used as a level. "But she's not the mother."

"But the receipt . . ."

"*I'm* Pauline McCormick. And believe me, the only thing I ever gave birth to was an album. You want Luba. She's the mother, but she's out shooting right now."

"I told you," whispered Maxine out of the side of her mouth. "Probably holding up a bank."

"She's an actress. She's got a role in this picture, *Witches of Wall Street*," continued Paulie, who may or may not have heard what Maxine had said.

"Who are you, then?" asked Bradley, who was trying to get a better picture of what was going on here and just who his baby's mother was.

"I was the father before you," replied Paulie, a little ironic grin playing at the corners of her mouth.

"Oh," was all Bradley could think of to say. He thought he had a pretty good picture now of what was going on. He felt his face begin to tinge with red.

"So how's the kid?" inquired Paulie.

"The baby's just fine . . . now," answered Maxine.

Paulie picked up on the "now." "Now? What happened to him?"

"I had to take him to the hospital," said Bradley.

"That's why we're here," added Maxine.

Paulie looked from one to the other and shrugged. "I don't have a medical plan. But if you need some money . . ."

"No, no, it's not that. We need to get some information about the baby. Birth weight, age, medical history." Maxine ticked off the list on the end of her still-gloved fingers.

"And we need his birth certificate," added Bradley, "for when he goes to school."

"School? You uptown types like to plan ahead, don't you?" Paulie laughed and relaxed a little. Her initial thought when she heard Maxine mention Rogue over the intercom was that they wanted to give the baby back, so she had decided to play dumb. She knew that Luba didn't want the baby back. And had in fact signed a three-picture deal with TriStar only yesterday. The kid's acting career was starting to take off. Probably because she had done what Paulie said and let her white-picket-fence side show through. With the right handling she could go far as the next Little Miss Middle America, especially now she had got rid of the pink hair, the mesh stockings and the army boots.

Paulie stood up. "Listen, I got a session in a few minutes and Luba won't be home til later."

Maxine took the hint and stood up also. Bradley followed suit. Paulie continued, "But I'll tell her you guys dropped by and I'll get her to get all the stuff she has about the baby together and get it to you, O.K.?"

"Fine," said Maxine, grateful that Paulie hadn't asked them to wait. It was getting dark outside and she didn't like the idea of trying to get a cab "down here" in the dark. It would be bad enough in the daylight.

Paulie walked the two of them to the top of the stairs. Then she turned to Bradley. "So, how do you like being a father?"

"I think I like it," answered Bradley with youthful candor.

Paulie nodded her approval and then turned to Maxine. "You're Dear Maxine, right?"

Maxine nodded, surprised. Though come to think of it, from the letters she had been getting lately she shouldn't have been all that surprised that her audience included the Paulies and the Lubas of the world.

Paulie clapped her on the shoulder. "Luba'll be pleased her kid went to Dear Maxine's son. She reads your column every month. Quotes you all the time."

"She does?" replied Maxine, flattered in spite of the source.

"Yeah, are you kidding? She thinks you've got the answers for everything. That's why when you said that it was O.K. for that woman who wanted to concentrate on her career to give her baby back to her ex-husband in last month's column, Luba knew it would be O.K. to give Rogue back to his father. 'Course, we didn't know you were going to turn out to be his grandmother." Paulie laughed, showing off a row of perfect white teeth set in a bas relief of brown nicotine stains. "Life's a riot, ain't it!" And she clapped Maxine once more on the shoulder.

CHAPTER FIFTEEN

HARRY WAS ON CLOUD NINE. He had to admit—and he did, at great length, to anyone who would listen—that although Joyce's pregnancy was certainly not planned, now that it was under way he was pleased, even—yes, he had to say it—thrilled. Something about making a baby at his age made him feel younger, more energetic. He no longer saw himself as on the verge of tailspinning off into the Decrepit Decades, doddering along the final highways of his life doing the senior shuffle.

For the first time in years he was thinking about the future instead of the past. It was a whole new mindset. And added to that was the fact that Joyce's doctor had told them it was going to be a girl. Or to put it another way, Rogue was going to have an aunt. Harry had never been the father of a girl before, so he just knew he was in for a whole new experience. He only hoped that Bradley would be able to handle becoming a brother after twenty-seven years of being an only child.

In order to break the good news to his son, Harry had invited him out for lunch. They had arranged to meet at twelve-thirty at The Chirp and Turf. Bradley showed up on time and Harry, who had arrived early because he was starving, waved to him from one of the booths, each of which was done up in a sort of wagon-wheel motif and ran the length of one barnwood-covered wall.

His son peered through the pale blue-white vaporous columns of cigaret smoke that punctuated the gloom provided by the hurricane-lamp light fixtures and waved back. Evidently the only no-smoking section at The Chirp and Turf was the alley that ran past the back door. Bradley gave a little cough as his lungs went on a pollution alert and gingerly picked his way between the formica tables and the captain's chairs with the red plastic seats, being careful as he went not to step on any of the work-booted feet that were extended in a sort of obstacle course.

The place was hot and busy and loud, and a fine film of grease clung to everything, including the air. Bradley looked around and noticed almost immediately that the source of this oleaginous blanket was located behind the counter, where a bank of deep fryers was being pushed to the limit by a man whose arms were completely covered by either hair or tattoos.

As he passed the counter he saw the man shake the accumulated beads of sweat and grease from his brow like a dog divesting itself of water after a bath. He shuddered at the thought of where these little bacteria bombs were landing and then plowed on through the murk. Whatever else it may have been, The Chirp and Turf was one of Harry's favorite restaurants, and since he needed his father's advice and possibly his help, he determined to grin and cough and bear it.

He slid gingerly onto the banquette opposite his father. On the table between them was a small ceramic chicken, which, judging by the contents that had dribbled and hardened on the outside, probably contained ketchup. Next to it was a cow of similar design that evidently did the same for mustard. Each place at the table, which would have seated four if Harry hadn't had some pull with the owner, was set with a paper placemat on which were pictures of the various dishes on the menu. And in between the salt and pepper shakers, which were actually converted beer bottles, there was a smaller sheet of paper with pictures of the beverages. Bradley was careful not to touch any of these.

"Hi, Dad," he said, leaning forward slightly so he could be heard above the raucous din.

"Hello, son. Isn't this a great place?" replied Harry, effusively smiling back. "Real food. Real people. None of that chichi bullshit in here. No siree. Just good hot food and plenty of it. And I'm ready for mine. Boy, am I ready. How about you?" And rubbing his hands together with anticipation, he looked down at his placemat.

Bradley glanced around the room. It looked like they were holding a casting call for a revival of "The Village People". He had never seen so many hardhats and cops all in one place. He understood why the menu was printed in pictures as well as words.

Harry looked up from the placemat. "D'you decide yet?"

"Uh, no, not yet." Bradley quickly surveyed the pictures of chicken and burgers which seemed to make up the bulk of the menu. "Uh . . . gee . . . everything looks so good," he murmured, thinking that he could really go for a nice endive salad and perhaps a little calamari.

"I'm having the Coop Combo," offered his father. "It includes wings, fingers and a burger. Why don't you try that?"

"A Coop Combo," said Bradley, slowly shifting the idea from his mouth to his mind and back again. "Mmm, sounds good." It sounded like it would be all fat and feathers. "Can I get a salad with that?" he asked hopefully.

"A salad!" cried Harry, sounding appalled. "What's up with you? You get fries. See, look at the picture." He poked a finger at the placemat. "You can't eat a salad with this stuff. All that grease'll wilt the lettuce."

Bradley decided to go with the flow. He had come here to ask his father for help with his life, not with his diet. And since this crowd looked like it thought DIET was an acronym for Double Icecream, Extra Twinkies, there was no point in trying to fight it. "O.K., Dad, I'll have whatever you're having."

Harry called over Guido the waiter, an even larger, hairier version of Tessio, the guy manning the fryers. "Hey, Guido, two Coop Combos and—" he turned back to his son. "What do you want to drink?"

"Alka-Seltzer?"

"Two beers," ordered Harry.

He turned back to Bradley. "So, how's the baby?":

"He's O.K., Dad. Ma's looking after him today so I can have lunch with you. Did she tell you we went to see the mother?"

"Yeah, lives down in Tribeca, right? With a roommate of the lesbian persuasion." Harry shook his head. "What a world."

Bradley nodded. "It seems that Rogue's mother is a thespian." Bradley had read the word in last Sunday's *New York Times*, and this was his first opportunity to try it out. He thought his father would be impressed.

But Harry, who was still in his what-a-world frame of mind, was only listening with one ear and half his brain. "Have you developed a lisp or something? I thought your mother said she was a lesbian?"

"She *is*, Dad." Bradley looked around to make sure no one was listening and then lowered his voice just in case. This was *not* the sort of place where you talked about alternative lifestyles. "But she's also an actress. You know, a *thespian*."

"A lesbian thespian?" Harry was having trouble keeping a straight face.

Bradley nodded. He had a feeling his father was enjoying a joke at his expense. "She's doing this picture called *Witches of Wall Street* and . . ."

That did it. Harry decided it was time to have his say. "Bette Davis is an actress. Katherine Hepburn is an actress. A lesbian thespian who works in a movie about witches on Wall Street is *not* an actress."

"Anyway, Dad," continued Bradley, who was not about to get into a discussion of the merits of intergenerational movie stars, "did Ma tell you about what happened at the hospital?"

"You mean about the nurse thinking she was the mother? Yeah. Kinda funny."

"Well," Bradley picked at the chipped corner of the tabletop, "it *was* funny. But it isn't anymore."

"How so?"

"This morning I got a call from the child welfare people. They think maybe they'd like to come and see me and my *wife*, make sure we're providing a proper environment for Rogue." Bradley heaved a deep sigh. "I haven't told Ma yet."

"It's getting kind of complicated, isn't it?"

"You can say that again."

But before Harry could, Guido the Large arrived at the booth carrying two foaming tankards of beer in one ham of a hand and two giant platters of cholesterol in the other. "Two Combos and two beers," he said, pronouncing it *Cum-bas* and *be-ahs* and slapping the whole lot down on the table almost simultaneously, slopping a good supply of the foam onto the formica in the process. "Enjoy it, eh, Harry."

Bradley wasn't sure if it was an order or a salutation. Either way, he didn't think it was possible. He wasn't really hungry and even if he had been, he sure wasn't hungry for this especially now he had seen it in 3D.

While Bradley was eyeing his food, Harry was busy slathering his burger with the contents of the cow and the chicken, on top of which he added the pickles and the container of coleslaw that had been snuggled up next to the bed of french fries that supported the wings and the fingers. When he had finished he looked up. He seemed perplexed and then his face lit up. "Hey, Guido," he yelled to the big waiter. "You got any chocolate syrup?"

Guido made an O with his forefinger and thumb and disappeared behind the counter. He showed up at the booth a few seconds later with a small dish of chocolate syrup, which he placed in front of Harry.

"There you go, Harry. Rather you than me, eh?"

"Thanks, Guido," replied Harry gratefully.

"No problemo," replied Guido, and he literally slid back into the fray.

Bradley looked at the dark, congealing pool of brown goo in the dish. "Dad, what are you going to do with that?"

"I'm going to eat it," replied Harry.

"Oh, Dad, please, don't tell me you're going to put that on your burger!" begged Bradley as he swallowed hard at the thought of the taste.

"Are you nuts or something? Of course I'm not going to put it on the burger. Jeez."

Bradley relaxed. "Thank God. For a minute there I thought—"

"I'm going to put it on the wings." And he poured the viscous brown liquid over the wings and dribbled a little more on the fries that lay beneath.

"Yuck!" cried Bradley, averting his eyes. "Dad, what's the matter with you? You can't eat that."

And then he watched as Harry devoured first one wing and then two, sucking the chocolate and the crisp skin and pale fat-soaked meat of the chicken into his mouth all at the same time.

Bradley grimaced. On top of everything else he now had to cope with the fact that his father was obviously a very sick man. So not only did he need to find a mother for his son, he also had to find a doctor for his father.

Harry wiped a smear of the chocolate sauce from the corners of his mouth and then picked up the burger and took a big bite, chewed, swallowed, had a mouthful of beer and then attacked the chicken fingers, which he dipped one by one in the contents of the cow.

Bradley, whose stomach had begun to squirm, reached out a hand to stop him. "Dad, wait!"

Harry looked up but kept chewing.

"Is there something wrong, Dad? Are you sick? Is it terminal?" Bradley's voice was full of fear and concern. He didn't think he could face gaining a son and losing a father in the matter of a few weeks.

Harry swallowed his food. "Sick? What's wrong with you? Of course I'm not sick. Do I *look* sick?" And he picked up his burger again.

"But, Dad, this food. The chocolate syrup. You can't be eating this stuff because you *enjoy* it. It must be some sort of metabolic imbalance. Maybe one of those weird digestive diseases . . . or maybe it's psychological. You know, a delayed reaction to the divorce."

Harry washed down the burger with another slug of beer. "I'm eating this because it tastes good, not because there's anything wrong with me." He thought maybe now was a good time to bring up his own little piece of news. "Has your mother been saying anything to you about what happened to me when she was pregnant with you?"

The sudden change of topic put Bradley even more off balance than the food did.

"Look son, there's something I wanted to tell you today." Then he stopped. He wasn't sure just how to put it into words. He cleared his throat. "When your mother was having you she got these cravings, you know. She wanted pickles all the time. And then after a while I wanted pickles too. Of course I've always liked pickles, but your mother and her doctor thought that the reason I wanted them *now* was because your mother was pregnant. Do you understand?" He looked into his son's eyes to see if the penny had dropped. But it was still up in the air, so he continued. "What I'm trying to say is that some men get like that when their wives are pregnant."

Bradley digested this information for a moment. "But, Dad, it's been a long time since Ma was pregnant. Why are you eating weird food now?"

Harry shook his head. When babies could be delivered in Bloomingdale's bags it was sometimes harder to remember the more traditional methods. He decided that the only way to deal with it was to come right out and say it. "Joyce is going to have a baby. You are going to have a little sister."

"A sister! You mean I'm going to be a bro—brother?" Bradley was trying to put this possibility into the proper orientation. He had come here to ask his father to help him find a wife and he was getting a sister instead. "Wow! Does Ma know?"

Harry nodded. "But she thought you should hear it from me." He paused. "Are you O.K. with this? I mean, is it going to bother you, you know, not being an only child anymore?"

Bradley thought things over for a few moments. When he was finished he looked up. "You know, Dad, fathers and sons are supposed to be able to do things together. Maybe we can be fathers together. It could be kinda neat."

Harry smiled at his son. "Thanks. I'm glad you understand."

But Bradley had gone beyond mere understanding. He was getting quite caught up in the idea. He leaned forward. "Yeah, you know, we can take the kids to the park and to the zoo and . . . You know, Dad, being a father is really a fantastic feeling. You're gonna love it. I know you will."

"I already do," mumbled Harry through a mouthful of french fries as he looked at the twenty-seven years of experience that sat across from him.

Bradley was so excited that he actually picked up a chicken finger and started to eat. It had a wonderful deep-fried, illicit quality about it, and it reminded him of the food he used to eat when he was a teenager, before he found out that everything but raw vegetables and under-cooked carbohydrates was bad news if you wanted to function past the age of forty.

Harry finished off his platter and burped contentedly behind his hand. "So, now we gotta deal with your problem."

"My problem?" asked Bradley, happily chewing on a chicken wing.

"Yeah, the child welfare people. When are they coming round?"

"God, I almost forgot! They're coming tomorrow evening. Dad, I've got to find a wife by tomorrow night or they'll take Rogue away from me. I know they will. Do you now anybody who can pretend to be my wife for one evening?"

"I don't run around with a lot of twenty-seven-year-old women, son. Especially not these days."

"Maybe Joyce could . . ."

Harry shook his head. "Even though Joyce looks younger than her age, I think in her current condition her pretending to be your wife would only complicate matters. I mean, she's four months pregnant and Rogue is only about three months old. There's a certain discrep-ancy there that someone from child welfare is liable to pick up on." He drummed his fingers on the table. "You know, there is someone you could ask. Someone who would fit the bill perfectly."

"Who?" Bradley took a bite of his burger. The flavour of charred meat sent his taste buds singing for more.

"Janie."

"Janie!" He almost choked and had to wash the meat down with a long slurp of beer. "You mean you actually think I should ask the woman who left me at the altar to pretend to be my wife? Dad, really, come on."

"You still love her, don't you?"

Bradley nodded. "You know I do."

"Well, my guess is she probably still loves you too. This might be a good way to break the ice with her. You know, call her up, explain the situation, play the daddy in distress. She loves animals, so you know she has a soft heart. I bet she'll agree to help you out."

Bradley was becoming more attached to the idea now. As it sank in, it didn't seem quite so farfetched. But he wanted to be convinced just a little more. "Do you really think so?"

Harry shrugged and smiled. "Does chocolate syrup taste good on chicken wings?"

After lunch Harry went back to the office. Not his office, however, but Maxine's. He had agreed with Bradley that he should tell her the news about the child welfare people while his son went to work convincing his ex-fiancée to play mother for a day.

When he stuck his head around the door Maxine was busy working away on next month's column and Rogue was in his usual place in the filing cabinet, sound asleep. It was a pleasant little scene, full of domestic connotations, but this time instead of reminding him with longing of all that had gone before it triggered only happy thoughts of all that was yet to come.

"Making up another letter?" he inquired with an edge of humor in his voice.

Maxine looked up from her work and smiled. Harry's presence was no longer an unwelcome blast from the past. Now that he was getting his own life back on track she found that she was actually pleased to see him. "No way. After last time, I have a whole new respect for truth in journalism."

"Yeah," said Harry, lounging comfortably against the doorframe. "It's bad enough to lie in print and lose a Pulitzer, but it's something else to lie in print and get a baby."

"I didn't *lie*," corrected his ex-wife. "I just rearranged some information. And anyway, *that*"—she gestured toward the open drawer of the filing cabinet—"proves that I was writing the truth, doesn't it? There are some mothers who want to give up their babies to the fathers. I just hope there aren't any more of them."

"As your editor I will accept that defense and as your ex-husband I hope so too. One motherless grandchild is about all I can handle at the moment. Which brings me to the point of all this."

Maxine cocked her head to one side.

"It seems that Bradley's little visit to the hospital is having repercussions."

"Oh-oh. I don't think I like the sound of that word."

"Like it or not, Bradley and his 'wife' are going to get a visit from the child welfare people tomorrow night."

"Oh no!" Maxine slumped a little in her chair. "But why?"

Harry shrugged. "It seems they want to make sure that Bradley and his wife are fit parents."

"Amazing, isn't it? Two women can have a defrosted baby together and then decide they don't want it. Nobody cares. My son was only trying to be a good father and all of a sudden the Kiddie Cops are coming out of the woodwork." She looked up at Harry. "What are we going to do? He doesn't have a wife. He doesn't even have a girlfriend."

"I told him to get Janie to come over and pretend to be the mother. You go out for a while and then come back and pretend you're visiting. You know, play the concerned mother-in-law. It would make it all look more normal."

"You're a sly one, Harry Kraft."

"Me? I'm not sly. I'm just being a father. You know he wants to get back with her. This is a good way to break the ice and make sure he doesn't lose the kid at the same time."

Maxine thought for a few seconds. "Maybe you and Joyce should come over tomorrow night too. Just drop by. You know, show the woman that Bradley comes from a loving family. Make sure it goes smoothly. It couldn't hurt."

"You're pretty sly yourself."

"Just being a mother."

Having solved that little crisis, Harry changed the subject. He had something of his own he wanted to say to Maxine. It was in the nature of a confession, and what he was seeking was in the nature of an absolution.

"I told Bradley about the baby."

"Which baby?"

"Joyce's baby," replied Harry.

"How did he take it?"

"Fine. He says we can be fathers together." Then he looked down, avoiding Maxine's gaze. He examined the toes of his shoes. They were scuffed. Then he moved on to the cuffs of his trousers. Was one longer than the other? Or was it just the way he was standing? He straightened up. There, that was better. Then, in a rush of words and without looking Maxine directly in the eye, he made his confession. "The-Rainbow-Room-opened-last-night-I-took-Joyce."

He took a quick peek at Maxine's face to see her reaction. What he saw surprised him.

Maxine had never been one of those women who could hide their feelings behind a bland mask of indecipherable expression. If she felt it, she wore it, in her eyes, on her lips, even, somehow, with her nose. And what she was wearing now said she was feeling a little bit sad, a little bit happy and just a hint of the bittersweet. It was a feeling he couldn't quite put his finger on, but the last time he had seen Maxine with this particular expression was the day Bradley had first gone off to school on his own.

"Are you mad?" he said.

"Why should I be mad?" replied Maxine with a shrug.

"Because I took her to *our* place."

"Harry, it's not *our* place. It belongs to the Rockefellers. And she's your wife. You can take her anywhere you like."

Women! Just when you thought you had them figured out, they hit you with logic, with understanding, with, with . . .

"Did she like it?"

"Sure. It looks a lot like it used to look, but different."

"Don't we all."

Harry got the definite impression that the subject had been dropped. He was off the hook and he eased himself off the doorframe. He was feeling relaxed and pleasantly full and forgiven. Things were coming under control and life was taking on an enjoyable if different direction.

Maxine noticed as he stood up straight that the material around his shirt buttons was stretched to its limit. "You're putting on a little weight?"

Harry looked down at his stomach. "A couple of pounds, maybe." He patted his belly comfortably.

Maxine nodded. "Cravings again, eh?"

"I don't have cravings. I'm just hungry lately."

"What did you have for lunch?"

"Chicken wings," replied Harry, and avoided going into any more detail.

"And what else?" prompted his ex-wife.

"Chocolate sauce," he mumbled.

"What did I tell you?"

"You know me pretty well, don't you?"

"We've been friends for a long time."

Harry nodded. That definition of their relationship had a comfortable, enduring sound to it. There was no finality. Unlike *ex*-wife, it didn't negate everything that had gone before. Satisfied, he moved to go. "Well, maybe I'll see you tomorrow night?"

"Probably. I'll be the one who's pretending she doesn't live there."

CHAPTER SIXTEEN

BY THE FOLLOWING EVENING Bradley had everything ready for inspection. The apartment was spotless. And the baby, asleep in Bradley's room, was clean, sweet-smelling and adorable-looking in a new pair of yellow sleepers that Bradley had bought that morning from a little shop just up the street called Yuppie Kids. But most important of all, Janie, who was the key to the success of the evening, had agreed after much coaxing and cajoling to come over and play wifie. *Not*, as she had pointed out to him numerous times, that she was not fully aware of the irony of the situation, *but*, if he was in trouble she felt it was her duty as a "friend" to help him out. And he had been so stupidly grateful that he had accepted her redefinition of their relationship without argument or comment.

But in spite of his efforts and his easy acquiescence to Janie's point of view, there was still one fly in the ointment. The child welfare people were scheduled to arrive at any minute and Janie was nowhere in sight. He knew this because he was standing by the window looking up the street for any sign of her.

He paced once, twice across from the window to the door, listened at the door for the wooshing sound of a rising elevator and went back to the window, leaving a nose print against the cold December glass as he tried to see even farther up the street.

Where was she? Maybe she only *said* she was going to come over when she actually had no intention of showing up at all, just to punish him for what happened at the wedding. Would she do that? Wouldn't she? How could she do that after all they'd been through together? Maybe that was why.

He went down the hall and listened outside the bedroom door for the sound of a stirring baby. Nothing. Well at least that was something. If Rogue slept through this whole thing and the social worker was a halfway reasonable sort, he might just be able to cope without Janie.

He was on his way back to the window when a knock came at the door. Was it the lady or the tiger? There was only one way to find out.

When he opened the door, Janie was standing there, taking deep breaths of her own to offset the fact that she had obviously been hurrying. The tips of her ears and nose were red from their transit through the cold night wind and her eyes were watering just a little. Bradley felt a terribly compelling urge to reach out and wipe the wind tears away, but he caught himself just in time.

"You're late!" he complained, glancing up and down the hall and then pulling her inside. He was angry with her for not getting there earlier, but he was also angry that she had agreed to come at all. How could she help him out like this after what he had done to "them"? How could she make him feel so guilty and grateful at the same time? How could she say that she was just his "friend"?

"I *know* I'm late," she answered in a normal voice, slipping out of her coat as though she were just dropping by for a chat instead of a masquerade.

He saw that she was wearing the blue cashmere sweater and skirt, an outfit he had always liked her in, as he had told her many times before. It made her look so soft to the touch, so warm, so familiar, and so unlike the lady executive.

"Hush! You'll wake the baby," he whispered, taking her coat and being careful to avoid touching the soft warmth of her cashmered arm. He hung the coat in the closet. "They'll be here any minute."

"I'm sorry. I had to go to the opening for our new pet spa—Pet-

Ultimate. Do you like the name? It's going to be big, very big." Janie fluffed out her hair with both hands. It shone with dark red highlights in the glare of the hall light. "We already have people clamoring for franchises. We're offering massage, psychotherapy and exercise as well as your basic grooming . . ." She realized that she was babbling, but it helped to keep her mind off other things. Such as being in the same room as a man she was still in love with.

"I don't care if you're offering cosmetic surgery!" said Bradley. "I've got a problem here."

Janie regarded him with thoughtful silence for a second or two. It was a different Bradley who looked out from beneath the shining cap of brown hair. A Bradley who seemed to have grown older, or was it perhaps grown up? Anyway, she had the feeling that she was talking to a father now and not a son. Something about having the baby had changed him, and it unsettled her because she had not been part of his change. "Well, I'm here to help you with that problem, so the least you could do is let me finish a sentence."

Bradley could see from the tension in her jaw that this was not the time to stick up for his side of things. Janie was here. She was willing. That was all that mattered at the moment. Their old conflicts had no bearing on his new problem. He apologized. "I'm sorry. The pet spa . . . sounds like a terrific idea. Really. I guess I'm just a little rattled tonight." He took a deep breath. "I can't stand the thought that they'll take him away and put him someplace, with strangers . . ."

Janie softened a little. "That's O.K. I understand how you feel."

"You do?" Bradley was surprised by the honest commiseration in her voice. He hadn't really expected anything like that under the circumstances.

Janie nodded. "I know someone who feels the same way about his kids."

Now it was Bradley's turn to tense up. "That guy you've been seeing?"

"I'm not *seeing* anyone. And how did you know about him?"

"I just—" But before he could get any further there was another knock at the door. Loud, authoritative and very, very firm, as if the person who was responsible had a preconceived idea of what lay on the other side and already didn't like it.

"This is it," cried Bradley, checking himself in the mirror and running a hand through his hair. "Try to act like a wife, O.K.?" he said to Janie, although he didn't really mean it the way it sounded.

"If it wasn't for your little escapade, I wouldn't have to *act*," replied Janie, taking it verbatim.

And on that note, Bradley flung open the door.

There stood the brownest woman he had ever seen. She had brown hair, brown eyes, tan skin and she was wearing a brown no-nonsense business-type suit with a little brown bow beneath her Peter Pan collar. He could tell just by looking at her that her favorite season would be the two or three weeks between when the snow melted and the green and yellow promise of spring erupted forth. A time when the Earth was as brown and tan as she was and she could scuttle about the city on her missions of malice, blending in like a chameleon.

He also knew instinctively that she was the type of woman who went by the book. Even if the book was wrong. The type who dedicated her life—if you could call it that—to making the lives of others as difficult as possible, all in the name of helping those who were less fortunate than her. A very small minority indeed.

She peered myopically through her round horn-rimmed glasses, blinked her dead brown eyes and said, "I am Emmiline Crumm, from the Child Welfare Service."

Meanwhile, Maxine was on her way down Lexington to the all-night drug store at the corner of 49th Street, which blazed away through even the coldest and darkest of New York nights fulfilling every need from emergency prescriptions that could be a matter of life and death, to emergencies of a more personal nature, which, though less serious, were equally impelling.

Maxine had long ago discovered that she was a drugstore addict. Where other women might have spent their free time in dress shops or movie theaters or bars, she gravitated naturally toward pharmacies. She could, if given the time and the money, spend hundreds of hours and an equal number of dollars just pottering around one of these prescription palaces, buying a jar of this or a tube of that, sneaking little spritzes of cologne and trying out new shades of lipstick or improved brands of hand cream. It was no accident, therefore, that given the fact that she had to be absent from her home, she zeroed in like a homing pigeon on her home away from home.

Cheered by the bright lights and the colorful packages, and warmed by the rush of hot air that gusted down from the heater above the front door, she wandered up one aisle and down the other, happily examining the various products and periodically putting one into her wire mesh basket. She took her time, because she wanted to give Bradley—and hopefully Janie—plenty of time to convince the social worker that they were indeed providing a proper environment for the baby and plenty of time to be with each other in case there was anything they wanted to say—like "I still love you."

And so it was that after a while she found herself standing in front of the vitamin counter. She examined a few of the bottles, choosing finally a multivitamin and mineral supplement with calcium, and then edged farther along the display to the more exotic items such as Selenium, kelp tablets and Royal Jelly. Having no desire to eat bee food or seaweed, she moved over a little farther.

Lulled by the comfort of being in a familiar environment, her mind wandered as she tried to imagine what was going on right now in her apartment. It was a minute or two, therefore, before she realized that the brightly colored boxes showing pictures of sunsets or young men and women embracing upon which she was now focusing her attention did in fact contain not vitamins but condoms.

She looked quickly around to see if anybody was watching her looking at condoms, in case they misconstrued her being there as something more than accidental proximity. She was relieved to see that the nearest customer was across the store in the baby food section.

Casually, she looked back at the display. Not once in her entire life had she ever beheld one of these things during its utility. In fact, the only time she had come into close personal contact with one was at college. She had been walking past the men's dorm one day in her very first week and some overly lubricated freshmen had been filling containers with water and dropping them out of a third-story window.

One of these water bombs had just missed her. And even though it had exploded on impact with the sidewalk, there had been enough of its tattered remains left for her to see that it was more than just a simple plastic bag. It didn't take much to put two and two together after that.

And all the while she was married she had never given any thought to these things because she had accepted it as part of her responsibility as a wife to take care of *that* side of married life. But since her experience with the safety-conscious Jeffrey, she had found herself wondering now and then what she would have done if her evening with Jeffrey had gone on to its natural conclusion. Jeffrey had obviously felt that she was safe enough for him. But would he have been safe enough for her? To protect or be protected, that was the question.

She glanced around once more and then reached out and selected a box with a picture of a glorious sunset on it. She turned it over, read the back and found out that the product of this particular sunset was lubricated and that each of the individually wrapped contents came in a different color.

"They come in *colors*?" said Maxine out loud to herself. "What difference does it make what color it is?" She put the sunset box back on the shelf and selected a plain medicinal-looking blue box.

She turned it over and read the description. Lambskin with nipple. She pulled a face. "I'll never feel the same way about lamb chops again." And she put that box back next to its contemporaries.

The next box was the one showing the couple embracing. They looked young, they looked happy. They looked Japanese? No, wait. Maxine took a closer look. You couldn't really tell what nationality they were. In fact, she wasn't even sure now that she was really *looking* at them that they were even of opposite sexes. She turned the box over. On the back was an artist's rendition of the contents, underneath which was the word *textured*. "They make them like panty hose?" said Maxine in disbelief and slipped the box back onto the shelf. She was just about to move on to the next box to see what else it was she didn't know about condoms, when she heard someone coming. Quickly and without looking back she walked away in the direction of the baby food and the diapers. Now *that* was something she understood.

For the next few minutes she busied herself selecting diapers and handiwipes and oil, lotion and powder. But all the while at the back of her mind a little argument was going on. Part of her was saying that, with the world being the way it was, rather than leave anything up to chance she should go back to the condom counter, select the color, texture and material she found most appealing and buy a box.

Another part of her was arguing that to buy a box of condoms was tantamount to declaring her bedroom open for business. She was, after all, a single woman. And a single woman of her age didn't really need to worry about sex. Unless she met a single man. But even if she did meet someone at some point, maybe, how would it look if things got to the point of no return and she brazenly whipped a package of rainbow-colored rubbers out of the bedside table? What would he think of her? What *could* he think of her except that she was "ready." And the obvious corollary to that was that she was also "easy."

She carried on with this internal struggle for a few more minutes. Both sides presented their cases well, and in the end she decided to mediate the decision herself. It was very simple. She would buy a box, but she wouldn't use them because she would probably never need to. Her little coats of many colors would stay in the bedside table as a safety supply. It would be like having a fire extinguisher in the kitchen or a spare tire in the trunk of the car. It was just a little reassurance that in case of a sexual emergency, she would be prepared. Her mind could therefore rest easy in the knowledge that she was "ready" and her conscience could be salved by the understanding that she was not "easy." And besides, she wouldn't be wasting her money because one day, when Rogue was older, they could always make little rainbow water bombs and throw them out the window.

Satisfied that she had made the right decision, she marched back to the rear of the drugstore, rounded the corner at the end of the aisle that held the shampoo and cream rinse and tripped over a stroller.

She only managed to stop herself from falling by grabbing onto an arm that seemed to come out of nowhere. She staggered and regained her balance and looked up into a pair of worried blue eyes that rested beneath heavy salt and pepper brows in an open, intelligent face.

"Are you all right?"

Maxine continued to cling on to the arm. "I'm fine. Really. I should have been looking where I was going."

"No, it's my fault. I should be more careful where I leave this thing." He gestured at the stroller.

Maxine looked inside. There was a small blond-haired baby, fast asleep. She looked up at the man again. He was about Harry's age, maybe a little older. The baby looked like him. Another case of an older man taking one more shot at the gene pool. "Is it a boy or a girl?"

"A girl. Her name's Amanda." And he looked lovingly down at the tiny pink face.

Maxine nodded. Everywhere you went lately there were babies.

"Any my name is Vincent. Vincent Taylor. Dr. Vincent Taylor, if you're impressed by titles." He smiled warmly and stuck out one ungloved hand. Automatically, Maxine took it. He had a lovely deep mellow voice, and she couldn't help responding to his cheerful demeanor. He was the type of man that her own mother would have labeled "nice."

"I'm Maxine. Dear Maxine, if you're impressed by titles."

Vincent Taylor frowned for a minute and then it dawned on him. "You write that advice column?"

"That's me."

He smiled again and she noticed he had great teeth. Had probably been flossing for years. You could tell a lot about a man by his teeth. "My students are always bringing your column in to show me some of the letters you get." He gave a little chuckle. "Amazing."

"Students?"

"I'm a doctor of psychology. I teach at NYU."

"Oh." Maxine nodded again. This was the point of the conversation where it either ended or progressed to the next level. But, since Dr. Taylor obviously had a wife and family, there would be no next level. She looked around, wondering how to break off the conversation, since he didn't seem inclined to. In any event, she couldn't proceed on her original course because Vincent Taylor and his daughter were positioned right in front of the sunset boxes. And she wasn't about to ask him to move so she could take one off the shelf. Oh, no.

He followed the line of her vision. "Am I in your way?"

"No, no," lied Maxine. "I just came to get some of those." She pointed to the row of multivitamin and mineral supplements with calcium.

But Vincent, who hadn't spent twenty-five years teaching human behavior for nothing, looked into her basket. "I think you've already got some," he said, pointing at the bottle of vitamins and suppressing a smile.

Reluctantly looking down at the contents of her basket, Maxine felt her face growing pink. She had been caught being "easy" and she wasn't even "ready" yet!

"I . . . uh . . ."

"Why don't you try these?" asked Vincent, picking up a box of plain latex condoms. "They're not as fancy as some of the others, but they do the job."

Maxine felt so embarrassed that she wished the floor would open and swallow her right there in the drugstore. Here she was for the first time in her whole life contemplating the purchase of condoms, even though she never planned to use them—at least not for sex—and here was this man, a "nice" man, a man who under any other circumstances she would have been glad to meet, offering her some as though she did it all the time. As though she were a professional!

He held out the box to her and she stood there, one arm hanging limply at her side, the other clutching the wire basket as though it were a life preserver.

After an awkward moment, Vincent suddenly seemed to realize the position he had put her in. "I'm sorry. This embarrasses you, doesn't it?" And he quickly put the box back on the shelf.

His sensitivity to her emotional turmoil snapped her out of it. After all, it wasn't his fault she felt uncomfortable. "No, it's not that . . . it's just that I don't know you and—" Maxine caught herself making up excuses for something she didn't need any excuses for. "Look, the truth is that I've never bought these before and I just had to give myself a huge pep talk to get up the nerve to come over here and get some. And then here you were and . . ."

"Recently divorced?" asked Vincent.

"A little over a year."

"Me too." He nodded his understanding.

"What!" That was something she hadn't expected to hear. "But what about the baby?"

"My granddaughter. I'm babysitting while my daughter and her husband are at the Met."

"Oh." This put a whole different perspective on things. She wasn't talking to a married man about condoms. She was talking to an *un*married man about condoms. Which was worse. She looked around for an escape route, since the floor seemed unlikely to oblige. In her wildest imaginings she never dreamed she would be standing in front of the condom counter chatting with a single man about her divorce and listening to him pitch his favorite brand of prophylactic. This just wasn't the way you were supposed to meet men!

Vincent, who could sense her discomfort and incipient flight, tried to relax her. There was something sweet and vaguely naive about this woman. They were qualities you didn't meet up with every day, especially in women who were divorced, and he wanted to get to know this one better. "What about you? What are you doing out at this time of the night?"

"It's not what you think," said Maxine, nodding at the display of condoms. "It's just that I had to get out of my apartment."

"Had to?"

"It's a long story."

"I'm not in any hurry." If he asked her now it might scare her off. On the other hand, if he didn't, he might not get another chance. "Would you let me buy you a cup of coffee?" He half expected her to bolt for the exit.

Maxine thought for a moment. He was a nice-looking man. He wasn't a widower. He had a baby with him. And she couldn't honestly hold the location of their meeting against him. "That would be very nice," she said with as much casual aplomb as she could manage. "But would you mind having coffee at my place? There's something I have to check on."

He shook his head. "Not at all. Actually, I've got to heat up Amanda's bottle soon, so if you don't mind my coming back to your place . . ."

"No problem," replied Maxine, who was feeling quite relaxed now.

And she turned and started to walk down the shampoo aisle to give him room to maneuver the stroller around the corner.

"Wait!" he called after her. "Don't you want these?" He picked up the box he had put back on the shelf.

Maxine paused next to the L'Oreal. It was one of those moments of truth that happen now and then in life. One of those moments when you know that whatever you say a corner will have been turned and that afterward things will be irrevocably and forever different.

"Yes," she said firmly. "I do."

CHAPTER SEVENTEEN

JANIE AND BRADLEY WERE SITTING side by side on the couch, holding hands and looking the epitome of marital bliss. Across from them, in the leather wing chair, sat Emmiline Crumm, looking the epitome of a vulture in a tree. She had a notepad balanced on her scrawny lap and her pen was poised above the page as she asked her next in a long line of intimate and interfering questions.

"How long have you been married?" She read the question out loud and then looked up, penetrating each one in turn with her gaze.

"Six months," replied Bradley.

"Two years," answered Janie at the same time.

Bradley threw a panicked look at Janie, who picked up the ball. "Uh . . . well, you see, we've actually been living together for two years but we got married about six months ago." She thought it sounded like a simple enough explanation. She also thought it sounded like she was lying.

And so did Emmiline Crumm, but she wrote it down anyway and then placed a little asterisk in the margin to remind herself later where the largest gaps in their story had appeared. Not for one minute did she believe these two were married. She had interviewed a lot of married people in her time and none of them had sat together holding hands. Added to that was the simple and observable fact that the wife was not wearing a wedding ring. Whatever else these two may have shared with each other, it did not include a wedding licence. It was therefore only a matter of time before she caught them out in their lie.

"So you were pregnant *before* you got married?" asked Crumm the Inquisitor, directing her question at Janie in an attempt to put things in their proper perspective.

Janie did some quick calculations. "I guess so."

"In other words it was the baby which precipitated the wedding?" Crumm probed.

"Are you kidding? *Interrupted* the wedding was more like it," replied Janie before she could stop herself. "I—I mean, uh . . . yes."

"I see," said the social worker ominously and scribbled something on her pad. "Now about the baby."

"He's sleeping," offered Bradley helpfully.

"To be sure. But he should be awake soon, shouldn't he?" She checked the watch that hung off her skinny, speckled wrist. "It's almost nine. Don't you give him a bottle before you put him down for the night?" She addressed this last to Janie, again because her natural instincts as a meddler told her that the woman was the weak link in this chain.

Janie thought it might be a trick question. She threw a pleading look at Bradley, who gave a slight shrug in response. His brain was suddenly tongue-tied and, in the face of Crumm's interrogation, he was having trouble remembering anything about Rogue's routine.

Some . . . times," replied Janie, trying not to sound too indefinite.

And Emmiline Crumm wrote down "irregular feeding schedule" on her sheet of paper. Then she looked up again. "Now, Mrs. Kraft, before we get on with questions about the baby, I should like to ask *you* a few questions."

Janie nodded, unobtrusively swallowing the lump that was rising in her throat. Here we go, she thought. She wants to know if I'm a fit mother for a child I've never even seen.

"About the name. Don't you feel that Rogue is a little well, let's just say unusual?"

"Unusual? Uh . . . no. Well, maybe a little," said Janie, hedging and hoping that some sort of reasonable-sounding answer would present itself before much longer. Fortunately, one popped into her head at the very last moment. "Actually, you see, it's a family name." She smiled with relief at her response. That was a good answer. No one would question a family name, a name given by one's ancestors, a name carved from the trunk of one's family tree. Even if that name *was* Rogue.

"A family name?" Emmiline Crumm's mouth pursed suspiciously and a dozen little brown lines burst forth from her lips like the trajectory paths of exploding shrapnel.

Janie held fast. She was beginning to catch on to this woman now. It was all a question of not letting her intimidate you. She sat up a little straighter on the couch. "Yes, my great-grandfather, on my mother's side, was Colonel Mathias Rogue. He died at the battle of San Juan Hill." She decided that an unembellished lie was probably an unbelievable lie, but one that was dressed up in gaudy details might sound just false enough to seem real.

"He did?" asked Bradley, turning to Janie and looking amazed.

"Yes, *darling.*" Janie placed her elbow firmly against his ribs and exerted considerable pressure. "Remember I told you all about it, when we were deciding on a name?" Then she flashed him a look that said *Shut up or die.*

"Oh . . . ah, yes, I remember," said Bradley, easing himself off the point of the elbow. Then he settled down to be quiet. Something told him that Janie and the dragon Crumm would be the ones fighting this battle.

"I see," replied Emmiline Crumm, who was sure now that she was being lied to but wasn't absolutely sure about the details. After all, there *had* been a battle at San Juan Hill. "Now, uh, about your obstetrician?" She glanced down at her list of questions.

"Yes, Dr. Arnold Brewster," answered Janie without hesitation and looking the woman straight in the eye. She felt she was really getting the hang of this fantasy now. "A wonderful man. Really very, very good. I use him all the time. I mean—I mean I would definitely use him again."

Bradley jumped back into the conversation then to try to cover her slip. He didn't know about anyone else, he said, but he could do with a cup of coffee. Ms. Crumm flicked a dry tongue over her brown lips and agreed that if it wouldn't take too long a cup of coffee, black, would be very welcome.

Relieved to be out of the line of fire, even if only temporarily, Bradley departed for the kitchen. He knew things weren't going well and he had to get up and move around to dispel some of his anxiety. Also, his side was hurting him.

After a minute or two of listening to him banging cups and running water, Janie decided that she too needed a break from Emmiline Crumm and after making some asinine reverse sexist comment about men and kitchens, she joined him.

"How am I doing?" she whispered beneath the sound of the running faucet.

"I think you could have left out the piece about San Juan Hill, but that bit about Dr. Brewster sounded good. Who is he, anyway?"

"Chester's vet," replied Janie, getting the cream out of the fridge.

"Jesus Christ!" cried Bradley. "What if she checks it out? What if she finds out that your obstetrician is really a parrot pediatrician? Couldn't you come up with a *real* doctor, for Christ's sake?" His nerves were stretched tighter than Nurse McAdams's hair, and he lashed out at the nearest target.

Janie, who felt like the boy scout who gets mugged by the old lady he just helped cross the street, lashed back. "I'm doing the best I can. And you're no help. When I tried to explain about the name you acted like you'd never heard of Colonel Mathias Rogue."

"I hadn't!" cried Bradley, rapidly losing control.

"Couldn't you just fake it? You seem to be pretty good at faking things." Like many women, when faced with bald-faced logic, Janie resorted to cold sarcasm.

"What's that supposed to mean?" shouted Bradley, opening up Pandora's box and letting out all the unresolved hurt that had erupted at their wedding.

"It means that all the time you were sleeping with me, pretending you loved *me*, someone else was having your baby. You faked our relationship and now you've got me here faking being your wife!" Janie stood before him now, a trembling quivering figure of suppressed feminine fury.

"Nobody's twisting your arm, *friend*." Bradley spat out the last word as though it had only four letters, not six. He reached up and retrieved the coffee grinder from the shelf next to the stove.

Janie retaliated with her most effective weapon. Her presence. "Is that right? Well, what was I supposed to do? Let you lose the baby to Our Lady of the Tarantulas out there?"

"What the hell do you care?" parried Bradley, a typical male-painted-in-the-corner response.

"Well, for your information I do care. That baby cost me a marriage. And I'm not going to let something that cost me that much just slip away because you don't have the sense to have a wife!" And she slammed the canister of coffee down on the counter with such force that half of the beans jumped out of the top and scattered across the floor.

At that very moment, Emmiline Crumm, who had come to see what all the shouting was about, took one step forward. The sole of her sensible brown shoe was no match for a floor reduced to a seething mass of bouncing black beans. One support-hose-covered leg slid out in front of her, her arms flailed helplessly above her head, and for a moment she seemed suspended in midair like some sort of large flying insect, before she landed on the mass of beans with a crunching thud.

"Well, at least we won't need to use the grinder," said Bradley to no one in particular as he put it back in its place on the shelf and bent down to help the social worker to her feet. He knew the game was up now. Unless her brains were in her rear end, Emmiline Crumm could not be expected to have missed Janie's last comment about him not having a wife. No way.

But Emmiline Crumm said nothing. She merely dusted the residue of smashed beans off her skirt and, limping slightly, wobbled back into the living room. Janie and Bradley looked at each other and then, carefully treading over the beans, they followed her like two lambs to the slaughter.

* * *

She was sitting in her chair, stiff as a board, staring straight ahead. She said nothing, nor did she give any sign of what she had overheard until Janie and Bradley returned to the couch. This time they sat at opposite ends and not only were they not touching, they were not looking at each other either. *Now* they looked married. But it was too late.

Emmiline Crumm cleared her throat before she began her onslaught, and the sound of her rasping voice grated like sandpaper on their strained nerves. "It is very obvious to me that you two are not married," she began and then corrected herself in the interest of accuracy. "At least not to each other. And whatever your reasons for perpetrating this fraud, I do not intend to go into that now. My primary concern is the welfare of the child. And I want to know, Mr. Kraft, right now, where is Maxine Kraft, the mother of your baby?"

Bradley ran his tongue around the inside of his mouth to pry his teeth off of his lips and considered the possibilities of his answer. "Well . . . you see . . ." he began, but before he could go any further there was a knock at the door.

Grateful for the interruption, Bradley jumped to his feet. "The door," he cried, although it was obvious, and raced out into the hall hoping against hope that somehow the answer to his problems would be waiting just beyond the threshold. And to a certain extent his wish was granted.

After a few moments of scuffling and murmuring, which both Janie and Ms. Crumm strained their ears to decipher, he reappeared, followed by Maxine, Dr. Vincent Taylor and the tiny, pink Amanda.

Emmiline Crumm looked this trio up and down, trying to place them somewhere in the family structure of the child named Rogue. They didn't fit. And yet they were obviously a part of whatever was going on here. This she could tell because two of the three of them were trying hard not to look as if anything out of the ordinary was going on, which meant that they knew just the opposite to be the case.

Bradley made the introductions. "This is, ah, my mother," he said, purposely leaving out her name. "And this is Dr. Taylor and this is Amanda," he said in an effort to explain as little as possible and still give the appearance of having said a lot because he certainly didn't want to give the social worker any more ammunition.

Ms. Crumm gave a perfunctory nod at the new arrivals. She would deal with them in due time. For now she turned her attention back to the matter at hand. "Now, about your wife, Mr. Kraft."

"My wife. Yes. My wife." His mind drew a blank. Janie had obviously been discounted on that level and he didn't have any backups waiting in the wings. So what was left but the truth? He would simply have to throw himself on the thorny Ms. Crumm—only in the verbal sense, of course—and hope she understood that just because there was a baby didn't mean there had to be a wife. He threw his hands up in the air in a gesture of helpless surrender. "I don't have a wife."

"Ah-hah!" cried Crumm, fixing him with one pointed finger. "You don't have a wife? But you do have a baby. Is that correct?"

Bradley thought that Crumm, who had the uncanny knack of reducing weeks of upheaval to two simple sentences, should have been a politician or one of those people who abridges books for *Reader's Digest*. But he nodded.

"Then who is Maxine Kraft?"

"I am Maxine Kraft," replied Maxine. If her son was going to confront this dragon with the truth then she would help him.

Emmiline Crumm focused her attention on Maxine. "And what is your relationship to the child, if any?"

"I am the mother of the father," replied Maxine, calmly.

Crumm wrote that down and turned her attention to Vincent Taylor. "And are you also related to the father?"

"No," replied Vincent in all honesty as he cuddled Amanda. "Actually, I am the father of the mother."

He had come up against women like this before, both professionally and personally. Anal retentive personalities combined with feminist ideology—a loaded combination and a sign of the times. They were totally incapable of accepting the viability of even the smallest deviation from the traditional nuclear family, especially when fathers somehow acquired custody, a plot they assumed was directed at making women, that is mothers, totally obsolete and therefore removing the final source of their power over men. He did not appreciate either their attitude or their point of view.

So when Maxine had filled him in on the particular deviations of her own nuclear family on the way back from the drugstore, and since his own fractured family was also far from the norm, he had determined therefore to resist facilitating the social worker's job if possible, though without actually reconstruing the facts, because that would be a violation of his professional ethics.

The social worker dutifully wrote down what he had said, although she had no idea whether the mother he purported to be the father of was related to the baby he was holding or the one she was investigating. "And is that your baby?" She pointed at Amanda.

"No," replied Vincent, offering no further explanation and slipping the toothless Amanda a knuckle to rub against her burgeoning gums.

"I see," replied Emmiline Crumm, although she didn't. She felt she was getting more and more confused. And again she wrote something down on her notepad. It was in fact a sort of player's guide that she could refer to as her interview progressed and thereby keep everything and everyone in order. "One doctor, two babies, one father, one grandmother, and no mothers. And two women both espousing some claim to being a Mrs. Kraft." Now at least she knew who she was dealing with.

Before she could proceed any further with her interrogation, however, there was another knock at the door. Once more Bradley leaped to his feet. "Door," he cried again with just a hint of hysteria and returned to the hallway.

He was back a few seconds later, herding his father and the obviously pregnant Joyce into the living room, which was by this point getting pretty crowded. He went to introduce them, but Emmiline Crumm cut him off. "I'll do it, if you don't mind," she said and turned her lizardlike lips in the direction of the newcomers.

"And you are?"

Harry, who was a little taken aback by the crowded state of his former living room and the presence of a strange man and a baby he had never laid eyes on before plus Lucy the Lizard Lady, who in no way resembled his idea of a woman bound by empathy and social concern to ease the lot of those over whom she had power, decided to answer anyway. "I am Harry Kraft."

"And what is your relationship to this man and his child?" She waved a clawlike hand at Bradley.

"Uh . . . I am the father of the father," replied Harry, looking around the room for confirmation that he had given the *right* answer, even though he had only uttered the truth. Maxine gave him a barely perceptible nod. Emmiline Crumm was going to find out that she was not the only one who could make things difficult.

Satisfied, Crumm then turned to Joyce, but before she could ask the question, Joyce volunteered. "I am the wife of the father," she replied, falling easily into the parlance of the evening and wondering if perhaps this was some sort of familial version of "What's My Line?"

The social worker looked from one to the other and, muttering something under her breath, she amended her list. "*Three* Mrs. Krafts, two fathers, two-and-a-half babies, one grandmother and one doctor." Something fishy was going on here. No doubt about it.

"Before we go any further, would anyone like some coffee?" It was Maxine, who had not yet seen the state of the kitchen, who made the offer in an attempt to give everyone a chance to think about what they were going to say before they said it.

"I'll have a Scotch, double," replied Harry before anyone else could get a word in.

"Milk for me," said Joyce, running a soothing hand around the perimeter of her stomach, which now that she was sitting down made it look as though she was hiding a basketball under her dress.

"Vincent?" asked Maxine.

"A glass of wine would be nice. And do you have somewhere I could heat the bottle? It's almost time for her last feeding."

Maxine raised her eyebrows in the direction of the wing chair, but Emmiline Crumm shook her head. Beverage-wise, she was determined to quit while she was ahead.

"I'll help you clean up the mess," said Janie, glad of something productive to do now that her role as wife had been cut to a mere guest appearance.

"What mess?" asked Maxine, following her into the kitchen.

When they had gone, the social worker stood up. "I would like to see the baby *now*, Mr. Kraft."

Both Bradley and Harry stood up, and then Harry, realizing his mistake, sat down again with a sheepish grin.

"I'll go and get him," said Bradley quietly, and he disappeared down the hall. Rogue, unaware that his future was hanging in the balance, was still asleep. And even as Bradley picked him up out of the laundry basket and wrapped him in a blanket, he slept on. Bradley stood holding him for a few minutes, listening to the beat of his tiny heart and vowing silently that whatever happened he was not going to give up this baby to that woman. Then he returned to the living room.

Emmiline Crumm immediately reached out and took Rogue in the thin tubes of her arms. She moved aside the blanket and looked down into his face. To her practiced eye he seemed clean and well cared for. But that was not the point. She now had to find out just who among this gathering—if any—were his parents. Otherwise she was duty-bound to take the child into the custody of the State of New York for its own protection until his parentage could be established.

As she was examining the baby, Vincent returned with a suckling Amanda busily gulping down the warmed contents of her bottle. He sat down and Maxine placed his drink next to him on the end table. The she put down Harry's Scotch and passed Joyce her milk and went back to the kitchen to get a bottle ready for Rogue. Janie returned to her place in exile at the far end of the couch. It was a full house and Bradley, realizing that they were now out of chairs and that this might turn into a long night, went to retrieve one from his room.

It took Emmiline Crumm only a few moments to discover that she could not take notes and hold a baby at the same time. So she looked around for someone with an empty lap. Her natural suspicion of men caused her to pass by both Bradley, who had just returned with his chair, and Harry, who nursed his Scotch while he watched the strange man nurse his strange baby on *his* old couch. And since Maxine was still in the kitchen and Joyce no longer had a lap to speak of, she went to hand the baby to Janie.

Janie, who was sitting stonily at the far end of the couch feeling hard done-by and partly invisible, was surprised by the sudden thrusting of a warm bundle into her arms.

"Hold him until I finish," ordered Crumm.

"Do I have to?" replied Janie, taking the bundle reluctantly. The last thing she wanted to do was to hold the child of the man she had almost married. To be reminded that this little bundle that stood between her and the man she loved was not just an inconvenience, not just a lump in a shopping bag, not just *the baby*, a faceless noun—but Bradley's baby.

A funny feeling came over her as she took him in her arms. A feeling that she knew if she were not careful it could undermine her decision and cause her to accept a situation that she knew she could not live with. Damn! But in spite of her aversion to holding him and her knowledge of the possible risk involved, she still had an overwhelming urge to open the flap of the blanket and take a look at the tiny face. To follow the natural urge of women everywhere to trace the images of loved ones on the faces of the newly born. But, with the stubborn determination of one who never reneges on a promise or tempers a decision, she fought it off.

Except for the nursing noises of the contented Amanda and the occasional mewing noises from underneath Rogue's blanket, the room was absolutely silent for a few moments as everyone looked at everyone else and tried to determine what the best course of action was. But since none of them knew what had been said prior to their arrivals, all of them were trying to play the game with caution in case they put their foot in somebody else's mouth.

Crumm, meanwhile, was busy scribbling on her pad.

Suddenly the symphonic scratching of her pen was usurped by yet another knock at the front door.

"I'll get it," cried Bradley, who was getting used to this but who was also running out of family at this point and couldn't fathom for the life of him who it could be.

A few eyebrows threw questions around the room like some sort of silent jungle telegraph. But no one else seemed to have any idea who it could possibly be either. All heads turned slightly toward the doorway in anticipation of the newcomer.

In a few moments a young, striking-looking girl entered the room. She looked fresh-faced and starry-eyed and bore a somewhat remarkable resemblance to Mary Pickford—though in a much more modern cast, of course.

"*This* is Rogue's mother," exclaimed Bradley, who had managed to ascertain that much at the door, although at first he didn't believe her because she looked nothing like the girl who had dropped his son off at the synagogue. "She came to bring me the birth certificate." And he held up the prize in his left hand. Somehow his prayers had been answered. The day had been saved. And just in the nick of time.

"Hi, everybody," cried Luba, waving one hand at the assembled masses and flashing her best 8x10 smile.

Emmiline Crumm growled audibly and amended her notes one more time. "*Four* Mrs. Krafts, two fathers, two-and-a-half babies, one grandmother, one doctor." Then she looked up from her pad.

"I am going to get to the bottom of what is going on here, if it takes all night," she warned. "Now, you two." She pointed to Maxine and Vincent. "Are you married?"

Maxine kept a straight face. "No, we're divorced."

Vincent barely held back a smile, turning it into a yawn. "Pardon me. Must be getting late."

But Crumm, who may have been confused but was not stupid, was catching on. She knew she would get no cooperation from this group of urban gypsies. "From each other?" she added cagily.

"No," replied Maxine. "I'm divorced from him." She nodded at Harry.

"Then what is your relationship to *him*?" persisted Crumm as she pointed at Vincent.

"None. I just met him at the condom counter in the drugstore. You know, the one at 49th and Lexington. So naturally I invited him home for coffee," replied Maxine, giving her best wide-eyed, doesn't-everybody-do-this? expression.

"*Harrump!*" replied Crumm and wrote it down. It was obvious to her that these people were not the kind of people who should be looking after *one* baby, never mind two-and-a-half babies.

When she looked up again she directed her attention to Luba, who was sitting demurely in the chair that Bradley had retrieved from his bedroom.

"You say you are the mother of the baby named Rogue?"

"That's right," answered Luba, trying hard to be helpful because Paulie had told her about the visit from Dear Maxine and her son and she was very impressed to think her child was the grandchild of a woman who knew all the answers.

"Are you and the father," she indicated Bradley, "married or do you live together?"

"No, we've never met before," replied Luba with a bright smile.

"You've never *met* before?" Crumm repeated her answer in case she might have misheard it the first time.

Luba shook her head, bright golden curls dancing like bubbles on top of her shoulders.

"So you've never been married or lived together or—?"

"Nope. I live with Paulie," she said, hoping to make it easier for this odd-looking brown woman to understand the situation.

Crumm's jaw tensed visibly. She scrutinized the assembled to refresh her memory. There was no Paulie among them. "And who is Paulie?"

"Don't ask," warned Maxine.

But Crumm persisted. "Who," and she looked threateningly at them all, "or *what*, is Paulie?"

"Paulie is my girlfriend."

"I see. And in what sense of the word do you mean *friend*?" Crumm felt she was getting down to the nitty gritty now, and it was very gritty indeed.

Now it was Harry's turn to interrupt. This woman was really beginning to piss him off and he intended to give her a piece of his mind. The only problem was the Scotch had twisted his tongue a little. "For Christ's sake," he cried, thumping his free hand on the arm of the couch, "don't you get it? She's a thespian!"

"A thespian!" the rest of them chorused, swiveling their heads to look at Harry.

Luba looked confused. She bit her bottom lip. "That's not what we call it."

"Well, what do *you* call it?" Crumm was gritting her teeth and sitting on the edge of her chair now, pen poised like a dagger over the page.

"Paulie's a lesbian," said Luba.

"I told you not to ask," said Maxine with a certain amount of satisfaction.

"And you're not a lesbian?" inquired the social worker, who wanted to make sure she had the facts, ma'am, just the facts.

"Oh, no," giggled Luba with a high-pitched little trill. "I go both ways."

"I need a drink," muttered Bradley, and he stumbled out into the kitchen.

"I could use a refill," called Harry, waving his glass in the direction of the doorway.

Bradley returned a moment later carrying the bottle of Scotch, slopped some into his father's proffered glass and then raised the bottle to his lips.

Luba, unabashed about the content of her testimony, leaned over toward Joyce, who happened to be sitting nearest to her chair. "Who is that woman?" she whispered, cocking her head at Emmiline Crumm, who was now making deep gouges in her notepad with the tip of her pen.

"Child Welfare," whispered Joyce, raising her eyebrows for emphasis.

"Oh," Luba nodded understandingly and then added, "I didn't know babies could get welfare."

Joyce's groan was barely audible.

Vincent was taking it all in. All he had wanted was a cup of coffee and a nice chat with an interesting and attractive woman. As it was, it looked like he had the makings of an interesting paper to present before the APA at their next meeting. If only they gave Nobel Prizes for psychology he would be a definite contender if he wrote up what he was now observing. He could almost see the title: "The Coping Mechanisms of the Urban Family in a Multi-Dimensional Extended Unit, Under Intervention."

Getting bored with all the writing and drinking and no longer being the center of attention, Luba leaned sideways again and said, "You're pregnant."

"You're kidding," said Joyce, shifting her weight to get a little more comfortable.

"Did you get yours from him too?" Luba waved her long white fingers at Bradley, who, oblivious to the consequences, was just taking another swig from the Scotch bottle.

Joyce rolled her eyes to the ceiling and shook her head. "No. Same family, different vintage."

"Oh," replied Luba, crinkling up her forehead. She had had no idea that sperm was dated the same way as wine.

Janie, meanwhile, was busy having a good long look at the mother of Bradley's child, an act that women are wont to do with possible rivals. After a few minutes and sexual proclivities aside, she decided she had nothing to worry about. Whatever the woman might have had going for her in the looks department, she lacked in the brains department.

Just then, Rogue stirred in her arms. He stretched one pink fist out from beneath the blanket, kicked his legs and let out the deep, deep sigh of an awakening infant. Now that he was awake, no longer simply a warm weight in her arms, she could not resist the urge to take a look at him. She folded the corner of the blanket back and held the tiny body slightly away from her so she could get a better look at Bradley's son. And as she did so she experienced the unmistakable feeling that the gears that guide the revolutions of the planet were grinding abruptly to a halt. In a mere millisecond, the earth, as they say, stood still.

"Oh my God!" The first time she formed her lips around the words no sound came out. The second time it did. "*Oh my God!*"

Emmiline Crumm stopped writing. Maxine came rushing in with a half-warmed bottle of formula. Vincent stopped tilting Amanda's bottle and she started to choke. Harry, who was just about to take a sip of his Scotch, swallowed the whole thing instead. And Bradley, who had been hanging around in the background trying to decipher the truth so he could confess his circumstances to the Child Welfare Lady, the City of New York, the State of New York and Morley Safer, if he cared to listen, stopped doing all of the above and rushed over to Janie.

"What is it? What happened? What's the matter with my baby?"

Janie, who had had a few seconds of realization to get the wheels of her world turning once again, looked up and said to Bradley, "Nothing's wrong. But he's not your baby."

PART THREE

Is You Is,
or Is You Ain't,
My Baby?

CHAPTER EIGHTEEN

IMMEDIATELY after Janie's explosive observation about Rogue's right to bear the name of Kraft, all hell broke loose.

Emmiline Crumm, whose tightly wound coil of a personality suddenly slipped its spring, leaped to her feet, hurling both her notepad and her pen to the floor, and shouted hysterically, "I knew it! I knew it! You're running a baby mill out of this apartment. And you"—she pointed a trembling, vengeful finger at a shocked Vincent Taylor— "must be the doctor in charge."

"Me?—I—" stammered Vincent, who confessed later, when he could look back and laugh at all this, that he had no idea that a chance meeting in a drugstore was going to lead to his indictment for running a baby mill.

Fueling herself with her own fury, Emmiline Crumm then began hopping around the room flinging accusations and vilifications of this nature and that at everyone present and complaining about degenerates, men exploiting women, wombs for rent, and the price of theater tickets.

"Definitely anal retentive," sighed Vincent Taylor, realizing that as the only psychologist present, it was up to him to take charge of any situation relating to crazy behavior. He handed Amanda, who had begun to whimper at all the noise, to Maxine and stood up. Keeping a safe distance between himself and the raving Crumm, he circumvented the room and went over to Bradley, who was standing next to Janie repeating over and over again, "What do you mean, he isn't *my* baby?"

Janie, who had but a few moments before been unable to stop herself from blurting out her earth-shattering observation, was suddenly at a loss for words. She had spent the past few weeks getting used to the idea that Bradley was a father and that as such her own life would be forced to take on a new direction. Now, suddenly, she was confronted with the possibility that that may not be the case after all and the sign up ahead read not Detour but possibly only Dangerous Curve.

"Excuse me, son," said Vincent, gently prying the bottle of Scotch from Bradley's tightly clenched fingers, "but could I borrow this for just a minute?" And he took the bottle into the kitchen, poured a good measure of the contents into a water glass and returned to the living room, where he tried to get the gibbering Ms. Crumm to swallow some.

But Crumm was having none of it. What was going on here tonight was the scene and substance of her worst nightmares. Fecundity released in all its unbridled force. Women reduced to little more than walking incubation machines, ripening pods, slaves of the enemy sex who wanted to use them only as a means of conveying their gene structure into the next generation. She could think of nothing more disgusting! So when Vincent approached her with the Scotch, intent only on calming her down, she saw it as his way of reducing her to a state of helplessness and then creating another maternity slave.

"Nooooo!" she screamed, pushing his hand away, lather from her leathery lips flying forward like spume from a crashing wave. "Don't you come near me! I know what you want. You're not going to turn me into a baby machine too!" And with her dead eyes almost popping out of her head with fear, she fled down the hall to the bathroom.

"What? What did I say?" said Vincent, looking around at the others. He had no idea what Crumm was carrying on about. Never in his wildest dreams could he imagine her as any kind of a mother, unless you counted the kind that buried their eggs in the sand.

Slamming the door hard enough to make the pictures rattle on the living room walls, Crumm locked herself in the bathroom and remained there until the people from Bellevue showed up a while later to take *her* into protective custody, in one of those table-turning situations which prove that no matter how unpredictable it may be, life is never without irony.

"Wow!" squealed Luba, getting excited by all the pandemonium. "You people really know how to throw a party."

Harry, who had decided that the only way to cope with whatever was going on was to let the situation overwhelm him and run its course—much the same way as one did with a virus—looked up at Vincent Taylor and said, "If you're not going to drink that . . ."

And Vincent, glad to be of help to somebody, handed him the water glass. But before Harry could lift it to his lips Joyce took it from him and had a big sip. "Sometimes milk just doesn't cut it, you know what I mean?" she said, handing the glass back to Harry, who nodded his assent. And then she added, "Is this what they mean by the joys of family life?"

Bradley, meanwhile, was taking the news that he had been fired from fatherhood rather badly. "But he *is* mine," was all he said every time Janie tried to explain to him why she thought he wasn't. And even after she showed him the birth certificate where it listed the father as "donor unknown," he still wouldn't accept the possibility that she was right.

"But *I* was the donor," he insisted.

"You were *a* donor. Anybody could be donor unknown," replied Janie, trying to get him to deal with the facts. "You're not the only one who could have an affair with a plastic cup, you know."

But Bradley stubbornly shook his head. "He's my baby. His own mother even said so."

"His own mother has a bra size that's bigger than her IQ," argued Janie.

Still, Bradley wouldn't listen because he didn't want to listen. His whole life had changed since this baby had entered it and now to find out that it had all been for nothing was more than he could bear. He had lost the woman he loved. He wasn't about to lose the baby he loved as well.

But Janie persisted because deep down she knew she was right and with every minute that passed, with every scrutinizing look she took at the baby, she became more and more convinced that Rogue was not Bradley's son. Finally, in a last-ditch effort to convince him, she pointed out that the baby didn't look like either Luba or him. It had dark hair and a swarthy complexion, whereas they were both light-haired and fair-skinned. He began to listen.

"Maybe it's a recessive gene," he said, seizing on any possibility to keep his parentage in place.

"Not on my side and not on your father's either," said Maxine gently to her son. "Nobody in the family looks like that baby. Believe me. Your father and I always thought he must look like his mother—you should excuse the expression—but you can see, she's right here, and there's no real resemblance."

Luba, who had joined the little coterie at the end of the couch because it seemed like that was where the action was now that the brown woman had been taken away, did a 360-degree turn to prove the point. "I always thought he looked like Paulie," she said helpfully.

"Isn't it time for MTV?" asked Maxine pointedly.

"Is it?" cried Luba, looking around for the television set.

"But I *love* him," said Bradley, hugging the baby closer and closer as he realized he was losing the argument.

Janie looked up at Maxine. "Can I talk to you in the kitchen for a moment?" Maxine nodded and the two women disappeared into the other room.

"Are you really sure?" was the first thing she said when the kitchen door swung shut behind them.

Janie nodded. "I saw the pictures. Rogue is the spitting image of his father. And I know Steve went to the City Cryo Clinic too because he told me once he was going to get a surrogate mother and then he changed his mind."

Maxine hesitated before saying what was on her mind. She didn't think it was likely, but she had to be sure all the same. There was too much at stake here. "Janie, I've known you for a long time. And while I haven't always thought you were the one for my son . . . Anyway, that's water under the bridge. What I want to say is, we all know you don't want the baby. Are you sure that you're not just looking for a way to—"

Janie shook her head. "Maxine, believe me, I wouldn't do anything to hurt Bradley. I know how much that baby means to him. I wish I'd never seen the pictures of Steve's children. I really do. But you can't let Bradley go on thinking that Rogue is his son when there is a good possibility that he isn't."

Maxine thought it over for a minute or two. Janie was right. "Well, there's only one thing to do. Tomorrow, first thing, we go down to that clinic and we find out just who that baby's father really is and why that dingbat out there thought it was my son's baby she was carrying around in that shopping bag."

The next morning, just after nine, the two women arrived at the clinic on East 45th Street. Maria looked up from behind her desk as they came through the door, and her smile faded when she saw that it was two women and not two men who now stood before her.

The only women who ever came to the clinic were surrogates or women looking for a specific kind of baby to fit their lifestyle. These were quickly ushered out of the reception area, where they might make the donors nervous or, even worse, start up a potentially nonprofitable relationship with one of them, and into a room where thick folders outlined the physical, mental and creative potential of the sperm currently in inventory so they could choose the characteristics of the baby they wanted. It was something like shopping by catalog except of course there was no substitution and no sixty-day trial period.

However, Maria, who was a canny woman, could tell right away that these two women were not here to select a sperm sample or to offer to carry someone else's child. They were here for trouble.

"*Buenos dias,*" she said uneasily. "*En que puedo servirle?*"

"What did she say?" said Maxine to Janie.

"I think she said hello," replied Janie, who had taken French as her foreign language in high school.

"That's all?" said Maxine. "*Hmmmp!* Not only does my son have to donate sperm, he has to do it in another language."

Janie shrugged. "Maybe she speaks a little English."

Maxine turned to the woman behind the desk. "Do—you— speak—a—little"—she brought her forefinger and thumb within half an inch of each other to show what she meant by little—"English?"

"*Si,*" replied Maria.

"*Si.* That means yes," translated Janie. "She said yes, she speaks a little English."

"Then why didn't she say it in English?"

"Good point."

Maria wasn't about to give the game away just yet. She was a firm believer in the fact that you could find out more with open ears and a closed mouth than the other way around. And she was hoping that she could find out what they wanted before they found out that she spoke more than just a little English. Then she could be prepared to deal with it. However, her plan went awry because at that very moment Dr. Carter arrived.

"Maria," he nodded at the receptionist and then acknowledged Maxine and Janie. "Ladies."

"*He* speaks English," said Maxine to Janie and then moved to intercept the doctor as he was about to go through the glass doors into the clinic itself.

Ten minutes later Janie, Maxine and Dr. Carter were sitting in his office and he was explaining how difficult it was to get good help these days.

"You see, the receptionist we had before Maria—her name was Carmelita—very pretty girl. And, well, to be perfectly frank, we had a . . . ah . . . problem with her, relating to the, um . . ." He looked around for a way to phrase the situation that wouldn't offend his visitors. "What I mean is, ah, there were certain irregularities with the inventory control procedures." He looked at the two women to see if they had gotten the point around which he was circling with such verbal delicacy.

Maxine stared back. What did he mean "inventory control procedures"? What happened, they had a thaw? She leaned over to Janie. "What is he trying to say?"

Janie, who had gotten the gist of his explanation, tried to rephrase it for Maxine's benefit. "He's trying to say that there were shortages because the receptionist, Carmelita, was misappropriating the potential inventory."

"She was shoplifting the sperm?" Maxine was incredulous. "What for? She was doing a discount business on the side?"

"She was doing business on the side, all right, but it wasn't discount," answered Janie, and then she leaned over and whispered something in Maxine's ear just to clarify things.

"She was doing what?" cried Maxine. "Every day?" She looked across the desk at the doctor.

He could see she had a firmer grip on the situation now. "All day," he said, nodding his head for emphasis.

"*Oi vey*," muttered Maxine.

Then he continued. "So you see, we had a big problem. There has been a lot of demand for our product in the last couple of years. Single mothers, older mothers, mothers looking to have children who sing like Elvis or play like Menuhin." Then he got momentarily off track. "In fact, we had a sale on Elvis lookalikes just last week—clear out the old inventory, you know. Elvis is not as popular as he used to be . . . Now, where was I? Oh, yes. But generally we've had a lot of trouble keeping up with the demand for fresh sperm. It's like pasta these days, everybody wants it fresh." And here he turned to Janie. "So when Mr. Curtis changed his mind about the surrogate . . . Well, we really didn't see any point in destroying his samples, so we put them into stock, as it were."

"O.K., O.K., fine, I can accept that," said Janie for the sake of expediency. "But what I don't understand is, how did Bradley get involved in all this? He and the receptionist weren't . . . ?"

The doctor waved his hand to dismiss her question. "No, no. Mr. Kraft was always a very good boy." He gave a little chuckle. "I think he was planning on getting married or something."

"It turned out to be the 'or something.'"

"Ah, so you are the young lady." Dr. Carter nodded. "You are a very lucky girl. Mr. Kraft was a *very* frequent client."

"Too frequent," replied Janie, remembering the long, loveless nights before the wedding. "Now, can we dispense with my good fortune and get on with your explanation?

"Ah yes, where was I? Oh, that's right. So you see, we simply put Mr. Curtis's samples under Mr. Kraft's donor number. If you think that the baby may be Mr. Curtis's, you are probably right. A blood test will certainly help to clarify it one way or the other. And when the mother inquired about the paternity, she was naturally told the baby was Mr. Kraft's." He smiled. It was all so simple. Then he noticed the women were not smiling back. "We had to put them somewhere," he said, trying to defend the clinic's policies. "And please be assured that Mr. Kraft received the full reimbursement for these extra samples."

"I feel so much better knowing that," replied Janie.

"Good, good. I'm glad it's all settled. Now if there's nothing else?" The doctor stood up.

"But I still don't understand why you picked on *my* son," cried Maxine, who thought it was far from settled. This man obviously had no idea that a baby was a very personal thing, not just a test tube full of blue eyes or brown eyes swimming about waiting to be introduced to an accommodating egg.

The doctor sighed and sat down again. He had a baby business to run. Evidently these women did not appreciate that time was money. "Madam, it's really very simple," he said in tones of exaggerated patience. "Client numbers are assigned alphabetically. Mr. Curtis and your son both started coming to the clinic on the same day. They therefore have consecutive num—"

"Wait a minute," interrupted Janie. "K and C are a long way apart in the alphabet."

"You're right—in the English alphabet. But the letter K does not naturally appear in the Spanish alphabet. So Carmelita, whose attentions were not, shall we say, exactly riveted to her filing duties, simply put Mr. Kraft next to Mr. Curtis because they both have names that start with the K sound. Hence the consecutive numbers. And it was perfectly logical when Mr. Curtis changed his mind to just transfer the samples to the next donor number on the list, which was Mr. Kraft. Don't you see?"

Maxine looked over at Janie. She shook her head. "All this because there is no K in Spanish?"

CHAPTER NINETEEN

IT ONLY TOOK ONE DAY to get the results of the blood test. And it proved conclusively that there was no way Bradley Kraft was the father of the baby named Rogue. By then, though, Bradley had had time to get used to the possibility that instead of losing his son at the age of twenty-one he was losing him at the age of four months.

Janie and Maxine had both had long talks with Bradley, Maxine about the perils of parenthood and the vicissitudes of life, and Janie about a man named Steve who knew all about losing his children and who would no doubt be as thrilled as Bradley was saddened at having one more shot at being a father.

When both women were sure that Bradley was dealing, however shakily, with this newest turn of events, Janie put in the call to Steve. She didn't tell him anything over the phone. It wasn't phone-type news. But she got him to agree to come by Maxine's apartment at five o'clock by telling him there was something she wanted to show him. Steve wanted to know if it was a surprise and Janie said, "Oh boy, is it!"—leaving him in a state of suspended curiosity for the rest of the day.

Bradley spent the day with Rogue, working on saying his good-byes. Trying to patch up yet another tear in his heart, which, he reflected, was beginning to feel more bruised and bloody than Stallone's face had looked in any of the Rocky movies. First his bride, then his child. What next? The two women thoughtfully left him alone.

Just after five o'clock, Steve arrived. He looked ruddy and windswept from a day on his latest construction project and he smelled of cold, ionized winter air. Janie, who had answered the door, took his coat, and he removed his construction boots and padded in gray sock feet into the living room.

Maxine and Bradley were both sitting quietly beside each other on the couch. Both of them were curious to see who Rogue's real father was, even though Janie had already told them all about Steve, Steve's children, Steve's divorce, Steve's dog and Lavinia, Steve's . . . Well, there really hadn't been a good word to describe Lavinia, so Janie had dug around for a term from her Soc. 101 days and come up with *significant other*.

After the introductions were made and Steve had sat down, the silence resumed, since none of those who knew what was going on knew quite how to begin. And Steve, who smiled at first one face and then the other in the hopes of eliciting some sort of explanation for his presence, finally ran out of faces.

He looked down at his rough hands and picked at a lump of dry skin on the heel of his palm. Somehow, somewhere, in this group of people, lay some bad news. He could feel it. Though what bad news it could be he couldn't imagine since everything bad had already happened to him, starting with his divorce from Brenda.

Finally he looked up, ready for the worst. "O.K., I'm ready. You can let me have it now."

Maxine looked first at her son and then at Janie. "He couldn't even call it a him? And how did he know, anyway?"

Janie turned to Steve. "We didn't know you already knew. Did the doctor call you or what?"

"What doctor?" Steve scanned the faces on the couch again.

"The doctor at the clinic," replied Janie, frowning. She thought Steve would be a lot more happy than this at finding out he had a son. As it was, he was treating the whole business very matter-of-factly.

"What clinic?" Steve didn't know what the hell they were talking about. And then it hit him. "It's Tony, isn't it? Something's happened to Tony while I was at work and you called me over here to break it to me gently."

"It's not Tony," replied Janie. She realized now that Steve had no idea why they had asked him over.

"Who's Tony?" asked Maxine, leaning forward and trying to get Janie's attention.

"Tony is his dog," said Janie.

"I thought *Lavinia* was his dog," replied Maxine, looking at Bradley to get his consensus.

"No, Lavinia is his ladyfriend."

"His ladyfriend!" cried Maxine. "When you said she was his significant something or other I thought you meant she was a pet." The she turned to Bradley. "I thought Lavinia was a pretty funny name for a dog."

"Wait, wait! Time out!" cried Steve, placing one hand palm down over the raised fingers of the other. "Somebody please tell me what the hell this is all about."

"It's all about Rogue," replied Bradley, saying the name with some sort of paternal reverence.

"A rogue what?"

In the end Maxine took charge. "I think it would be easier if you just went and got him," she said to her son. And with a deep sigh Bradley departed to retrieve Rogue from his laundry basket. A few moments later he returned, and after taking one more longing look at the little bundle in his arms, he handed the baby to Steve. "He's all yours."

"What do you mean, he's all *mine*?" said Steve, settling the child in his arms and looking to Janie for an answer.

And she gave it to him, quickly, simply and with a minimum of explanation. That could wait until after Steve got used to being a father and Bradley got used to being the opposite.

When she had finished, Steve looked down at the baby. He had the stupidest grin on his face as he stroked the soft downy cheek with one work-roughened finger. "Wow!" He looked up. "I never thought I'd ever . . . I mean . . . You're sure he's really mine?"

Janie nodded, smiling at Steve's response. As much as it hurt to see Bradley lose "his son," it made her feel good to know that Steve had finally got what he always wanted and that Rogue would have a loving father to take care of him.

"What about Lavinia?" she asked a few minutes later, after they had all watched Steve cuddle and coochie-coo his baby and check all its fingers and toes.

Steve shook his head. "Lavinia! Jesus, I forgot all about Lavinia!" He grinned. "And she was worried about coming home to a litter of puppies. I'm going to have to do some fast talking to work my way round this one." He thought for a minute. "Maybe if I changed his name. I think Lavinia would have a pretty difficult time accepting a Rogue. But a Roger, now there's a name you can get used to."

"Roger!" cried Bradley. "But his name is Rogue. He's—"

Maxine laid a calming hand on her son's arm. "He's Steve's baby now. And if Steve thinks that someone named Lavinia will have trouble accepting the name Rogue, then he has a right to change it."

She was right, of course.

After Steve had left with the baby, the bottles, the basket and the new name, Vincent Taylor showed up.

"I never did get that cup of coffee you promised me," he said to Maxine when she answered the door.

When Janie saw who it was, and how it was, she decided there was no reason at all for her to stick around. "I think maybe I should get going now." She stood up. "Good-bye, Maxine, Dr. Taylor." And then she turned to Bradley, "I guess . . ."

"Do you mind if I walk you home?" asked Bradley, standing up and casting a sideways nod at his mother and Vincent, who were too busy looking at each other to notice.

"Sure," replied Janie, although she wasn't really.

Outside, in the accumulating dusk, huge wet floppy snowflakes were drifting lazily down out of the leaden sky, lending a thick white blanket to the trees and the street lamps and the fences and the odd street sleeper curled up over a vent. It would all disappear with the morning melt, of course, but for the moment New York City looked more like it was turning into the twentieth century and not the twenty-first. Somehow the snow had a way of covering up the ugliness and decorating the beauty of Manhattan all at the same time.

They walked along in silence, each lost in their thoughts. Janie thought that Bradley was probably thinking about the baby. And he thought that she was probably thinking about the baby's father or business or both. It never occurred to either of them that each was thinking about the other. After a time they reached Janie's house and they stopped at the bottom of the steps.

"Well, I guess this is it," said Bradley.

He had snow on his hair. Snow on his eyebrows and eyelashes. Melted snow running down his reddening cheeks. Janie nodded and turned and took one, two steps up toward the front door. Then she turned back. He was still standing there collecting snow like a statue in the park.

"I'm sorry about the baby, Bradley."

"I know. I guess it just wasn't meant to be. But Steve seems like a nice guy." He paused, gathering more snow. "You like him a lot?"

"I like him a lot," replied Janie. "As a friend."

Bradley nodded. He had the answer he had been looking for. He turned and took a couple of steps up the street. Then he turned back. "Maybe we could go out sometime," he said hopefully. Janie gave a little grin. "Why don't you come in for a while and dry off and we'll talk about it?"

Bradley hesitated. What was she offering? A few minutes out of the storm—or a lifetime? There was only one way to find out. He followed her up the steps and through the front door.

Chester, who had been snoozing on his perch in the kitchen, heard the click of the door lock and then the rumble of a male voice. He was immediately awake, all his keen bird senses primed and ready. He had been waiting for this moment for days. This time he was going to fire the first volley and dogs be damned! He stretched his wings, fluffed his feathers and took off.

Following a preconceived flight plan, he circled through the living room, preparing himself for the assault and then, when he knew he was ready, he sailed under the archway and out into the hall. Like a blinding flash of green lightning he hurtled toward the front door, his blazing orange eyes darting this way and that, seeking his arch nemesis Tony the Furball and his human, Steve.

And there, straight ahead, outlined in the dimness of the hall against the light that poured in through the front-door glass, loomed the large bulky presence of the man. Could the dog be far behind?

Chester soared to the ceiling, and hovering ever so briefly above his target, he released his load. "Bombs away!" he cackled gleefully, and turning on one wing, he sailed back triumphantly toward the kitchen, satisfied that his mission had been accomplished.

Bradley, who had just gotten out of his snow-sodden overcoat, suddenly felt a warm *plop!* on the middle of his head, a split second after he saw the flash of green feathers and heard the maniacal voice of the parrot. He had no doubt about what had hit him. But he had changed. He didn't care about a little bird shit on his head. Besides, it didn't only feel like bird shit. It felt like home.

Six months later, on a warm evening in early June, Maxine had just finished doing the dishes after dinner, and Vincent was in the living room trying to read the instructions on how to assemble a playpen, when the doorbell rang.

"I'll get it," he called getting to his feet, and Maxine let him. After all, it was his door, too, now.

In a few minutes he came into the kitchen holding Amanda and Amanda's teddy bear. "Jennifer and Mark said they'll be back around ten."

Maxine nodded. "She's getting bigger every day," she said, stroking Amanda's curly head. "How's the playpen coming?"

"I'm an intellectual, not an engineer," replied Vincent. "But I think I'm getting the hang of it."

"Good, we're going to need it."

As they walked into the living room there was another knock on the door.

"Right on time," said Maxine, looking at her watch.

When she answered the door, there was Bradley and, with him, the obviously pregnant Janie, the newly christened Roger Curtis, Chester, and something small, white and bouncy on the end of a leash.

"Hi Ma," cried Bradley, handing the baby to her and ushering Janie, the puppy and the bird in out of the hallway.

Maxine clutched the baby and eyed the dog.

"I hope you don't mind looking after the puppy, Maxine." It was Janie talking. "But you see, Tony and Marilyn managed to consummate their marriage in spite of Lavinia's attempts to keep them apart. Steven gave us their firstborn as a gift for looking after Roger while he and Lavinia are on their honeymoon. His name is Edgar."

"Edgar?" Maxine shook her head. "Whatever happened to Fido?"

Hearing his name and excited by all the new smells, Edgar immediately squatted and made a puddle on the rug.

"I'm sorry. I'll get a paper towel," cried an embarrassed Janie.

"Did you ever think about diapers for dogs?" asked Maxine watching the puppy pee sink into the wool.

"You know, that's not a bad idea. We could . . ."

"Ma, do you have to encourage her?" Bradley gave his mother a warning look. "It's bad enough she's got this Pet Cruise thing going."

"Oh don't be such a grump," said Janie to Bradley. "It'll be fun. People love to take their animals on vacation. Besides it's only for three days and we did say nothing over a hundred and fifty pounds or four legs."

"You could have said nothing unless it's warmblooded, like I asked you to."

"Oh Bradley . . ."

"Hello Sailor! Ship ahoy!" interjected Chester who was a much calmer bird now that he was able to take out his aggressions on the likes of Edgar whenever the urge struck him.

"Well, I guess that's our cue to say goodbye. Bye, Ma. Bye, Vincent," called Bradley to the figure hunched over the half-erected playpen.

Vincent waved his screwdriver. He wasn't sure if it was a Philips or a Robertson. But it might as well have been a wrench for all the help it was.

"Thanks for taking care of things, Ma. We'll see you Monday night." And with that they were gone.

Maxine, followed by the effervescent Edgar, carried Roger into the living room and placed him next to Amanda. The two babies eyed each other curiously and then Roger reached out and clouted Amanda over the head. She started to cry.

"Here we go," said Maxine trying to soothe Amanda and moving the babies further apart. Edgar took this opportunity to create another little yellow lake.

"Who's that?" asked Vincent pointing the handle of the screwdriver at the smallest new arrival.

"That's Edgar. He's Tony and Marilyn's son," replied Maxine.

Vincent nodded. Maybe we should put him in the playpen."

"I've got a better idea. Why don't you and I get in the playpen? It may be safer. It'll definitely be drier." And she came and sat beside him on the floor and watched for a few minutes as he tried to master instructions which had been translated from German to Japanese to English.

She looked around the room. It was the same living room she had spent the last quarter of a century in. The same living room she had shared with Harry and where Bradley had grown up. But all that was gone now. The man was different. The babies were different. Probably, thought Maxine, I'm different, too. But the room is the same.

"Vincent?"

"Hmmmmm?"

"Have you ever noticed that the more things change, the more they stay the same?"

Vincent looked up from his task. "No Maxine, I never noticed that." But he was smiling as he said it.